SPY PUPPETS

Spy Puppets is a spy thriller set in a small American town. Harry Starky, accountant to a Government Research unit, returns from celebrating his birthday to find the dead, naked body of Laura Nolan, a secretary at the Research Unit, in his bedroom. He also finds he cannot substantiate his alibi. Lieutenant Hugan of the local Police Homicide Division is put in charge of the investigations. With Starky becoming his number one suspect. What follows is a secret battle of wits between the FBI and an unknown master spy.

SPY PUPPETS

SPY PUPPETS

by

Geoffrey Davison

Dales Large Print Books
Long Preston, North Yorkshire,
BD23 4ND, England.

British Library Cataloguing in Publication Data.

Davison, Geoffrey
    Spy puppets.

       A catalogue record of this book is
       available from the British Library

       ISBN   978-1-84262-854-6 pbk

First published in Great Britain in 1973 by Robert Hale Limited

Copyright © Geoffrey Davison 1973

Cover illustration © Roy Bishop by arrangement with
Arcangel Images Ltd.

The moral right of the author has been asserted

Published in Large Print 2012 by arrangement with
Geoffrey Davison, care of Watson, Little Ltd.

Dales Large Print is an imprint of Library Magna Books Ltd.

Printed and bound in Great Britain by
T.J. (International) Ltd., Cornwall, PL28 8RW

ONE

Samuel Weiderman, a senior agent of the Federal Bureau of Investigation, thoughtfully read the reports from the untitled dossier lying on his desk. The contents concerned a Government research project being undertaken at the Chemical Plant in Medway Springs, Minnesota. A project which had been given no publicity and very little interference in the hope that it would not attract any foreign attention, but a Russian defector to the C.I.A. in Berlin had suddenly sent the alarm bells ringing. The Russians were not only very interested in the project, but knew sufficient of its progress for the F.B.I. Counter Intelligence Squad to be called in. Samuel Weiderman had been given the task of finding the leakage.

A call from Weiderman's secretary over the intercom interrupted his study of the reports. Senator Leebright and his assistant had arrived to see him. Weiderman frowned as he acknowledged the call. The Senator was not the man he wanted to see at that particular moment. The Senator was in charge of the Senate Sub-Committee responsible for the project. He was a powerful, influential man, who was becoming a well known national figure. But he also figured in the reports Weiderman was reading. He was on Weiderman's list of suspects and Weiderman hadn't completed his investigations of the man. But Weiderman knew that he couldn't refuse to see him. He carefully replaced the reports in the dossier and locked it away in a drawer before pressing a button on his desk which gave the signal to his secretary to admit the Senator, and his assistant, to his room.

As Weiderman stood up from his desk, the door opened and the Senator stormed into the room. Following in the Senator's wake was a small, dark, bespectacled man. His name was Julius Stein and he was often referred to, uncomplimentarily, as the Senator's brains. But it was the Senator who always demanded attention.

'Good afternoon, Senator,' Weiderman said.

'Afternoon, Sam,' the Senator replied gruffly. 'You know Julius?' He indicated his assistant with a vague wave of his arm. Weiderman knew the Senator's assistant, but the Senator didn't bother to wait to find out. 'Nasty business, Sam,' he grunted. 'I don't like it.'

Weiderman offered the Senator a seat. The Senator refused it and stood with his back to the window facing Weiderman. He had a Napoleonic stance and air about him. An attitude which he liked to cultivate. He was a small man, like Napoleon, but there the similarity ended. The Senator was slim, wiry, with a round, even featured face and grey hair, both of which reflected his fifty years of struggle to get to his present position. His features didn't look those of a dynamic, mud slinging politician, until he narrowed his eyes. Then people saw a different face – a face which looked determined and ruthless. He stood, hands clenched behind his back, his feet apart, and his eyes fixed on Weiderman. Stein, his assistant, stood somewhere out of the immediate vision of Weiderman, in the shadow of the Senator. A place which he always occupied so that he could listen and observe without becoming involved.

'I would have got here sooner, Sam,' the Senator said in his sharp, clipped accent, 'but I was out of town on business.'

Weiderman let the Senator's out of town business pass without comment although he was well aware of the nature of the business. Currently the Senator was barnstorming his way around the countryside trying, as the Senator put it, to get some fight back into the people after their setback over Vietnam. His platform was one of greater national pride and unity, but his speeches and tactics had a strong anti-Communist flavour about them. They also had a familiar ring. Many people remembered the witch hunt of the fifties and felt uneasy at the similarity of Senator Leebright's activities. Others who knew Leebright closely, and they included Samuel Weiderman, also suspected the Senator's motives. They suspected that all the mud slinging and dirt that the Senator was stirring up was just a means of getting the Senator national recognition. They suspected that the Senator had his sights set on the forthcoming Primaries when the Party would be looking for its Presidential Candidate.

'What do you know, Senator?' Weiderman asked.

'That we've been sold out,' the Senator said grimly. 'That the Commies have got on to the Cusack project at Medway Springs.'

'Yes,' Weiderman said. 'They seem to know quite a lot about it. They know that...'

'I've been briefed this morning,' the Senator intervened sharply. 'I've got friends in the C.I.A. I know how black it is.' His eyes narrowed. 'I'll take that Unit and Medway Springs apart,' he said. 'By the time Julius and I have finished with them they'll not know what's hit them. We'll flush them out.'

'Sorry, Senator,' Weiderman said apologetically. 'We'll have to play it my way.'

'What do you mean?' the Senator asked hotly. 'This has been my baby from the start.'

'Sure, I know, but I have orders.'

'Orders!' the Senator scoffed. 'Let me spell it out for you, Sam.' His face became flushed with emotion. 'It was on my recommendation that Cusack was given the Unit at the A.C.I. Plant in Medway Springs. My recommendation, Sam.' He emphasised his part. 'And do you know why?'

'Yeah, I know.'

'Cusack's research was a long shot,' the Senator went on. 'Nobody believed in the guy except me.'

Weiderman mentally sighed. He had heard it all before, from the Senator.

'I assured the Defence Department that there would be no slip up.' The Senator's

11

manner was becoming more aggressive. 'I have given this project my personal attention. Don't try and stop me now. I'll find the Commies. We've got a nose for them now, Julius and me. So have my men.'

Weiderman breathed heavily. Like the Senator, he could also be a tough man.

'Senator,' he said looking Leebright full in the face. 'I go along with all you have said, but,' he paused fractionally and added, 'I have my orders and they are from the top.'

'The top?' the Senator asked.

Weiderman nodded his head. 'The top,' he said. The two men eyed each other grimly. Suddenly Leebright's face relaxed. He knew he couldn't buck against the 'top'.

'O.K. Sam,' he said, 'we'll play it your way, first, but when you're through, Sam, I'm going to move in. This country needs a shake up and this is going to be it. There's too many people sitting on their fat ducks when the man right next to them is selling them out. I tell you this...' He suddenly stopped, and gave a disarming smile. 'There I go on my soap box again. Sorry, Sam.'

'That's O.K., Senator. We both have our own ways of achieving the same object.'

'Say, that's good, Sam. Yeah, that's good. Make a note of that, Julius. We must use that.'

The Senator waved his arm in some vague gesture to his assistant.

'What's the play, Sam?' he asked seriously.

'The Russians know so much about what is going on,' Weiderman said, 'that it must be somebody big. Somebody either involved with the project at Medway Springs, or...'

'Here in Washington,' the Senator added, his eyes lighting up.

'Yeah,' Weiderman said. 'Perhaps your committee.'

Leebright looked thoughtful for a long time. 'I know that committee, Sam,' he said finally with a trace of regret in his voice. 'I'll stake my reputation on them.'

'You're probably right,' Weiderman said diplomatically.

'Look for yourself, Sam. You take them apart and me. Don't exclude me, Sam. When this is over I can use the material.' The Senator had suddenly got a mental picture of himself on television telling the great American public how he had insisted upon being investigated to prove his loyalty. It made the Senator feel good. 'Now, I insist, Sam.' He didn't have to, Weiderman had already made his plans.

'Mind you, Sam, I'm not saying I don't have faults,' the Senator added.

Weiderman made no comment. He was aware of the Senator's interest in the dollies.

'After all, I am a bachelor.'

'I'll keep it clean, Senator,' Weiderman said, 'and confidential.'

'That's it,' the Senator agreed. 'How can I help?'

'McIntyre is in charge of the Research Security. He is one of your men,' Weiderman said. 'You got his reports?'

'He's a good man,' the Senator said. 'A good American. Served under me in Korea. A good man.'

'How are his reports?'

'He has kept me in the picture,' the Senator said.

'What is the picture, Senator?'

'Not as happy as it could be,' the Senator replied. 'They are a mixed bunch. The scientists work well enough together in the lab.'

'Not out of it?' Weiderman asked.

'Cusack is a Czech, Ludvick is German, and Kay is British,' the Senator said. 'Naturally they are not close.'

'What about the man in charge, Dr Logan?' Weiderman asked. 'You appointed him.'

'He spent a few years behind a desk right here in Washington,' the Senator explained. 'One of the advisors to my committee. A very good man. He needed the change and I wanted a reliable man in charge of the Unit. Logan's got a good record. He came from nothing, and made good. That type are reliable.'

'Sure,' Weiderman agreed without conviction. 'His wife had it easier,' he added.

'A Boston girl. Top bracket.'

'Played the society field here in Washington,' Weiderman added.

'She got about. They were popular.'

'You vouch for them?' Weiderman asked. He knew the Senator and Mrs Logan had been more than friends.

'Say, Sam, what is this?' the Senator asked. 'You asking me who I think is your man?'

'Who do you think, Senator?' Weiderman asked seriously.

'I wouldn't trust any of them,' the Senator said scathingly, 'and don't you. You'll get my support and help. I'm with you all the way.'

'Thank you, Senator,' Weiderman said. 'If you will just let me have McIntyre's reports as soon as possible.'

'Make a note of that, Julius,' the Senator called out to his assistant. He turned his attention back to Weiderman. 'Now I have to get back to my other business,' he said. His mouth twisted into a self satisfied smile.

15

'We've made a lot of people sit up and take notice,' he said proudly. 'I tell you this…'

The Senator got on to his hobby horse again. Weiderman caught sight of the date on his desk calendar – 2nd June – and immediately thought of the Research Centre at Medway Springs. He knew that the date was significant for one of the key personnel at the Centre. Now who was it again? he wondered. Who was it? He mentally went through the names. There was Logan in charge, McIntyre the Security Officer; the four scientists – Cusack, Ludvick, Kay and Benson; Mrs Bradley the Statistician and Records Officer, and Starky the Accountant. Starky! he thought – Harry Starky. It was Starky. Now what was that?…

TWO

Harry Starky looked at himself in the cracked, tinted mirror which faced him and saw his round, open face and sleek black hair. He gave a grunt of satisfaction and took another long drink. There was no one to question his action because he was drinking alone and he wanted it that way. Harry Starky had purposely gone to Luigi's saloon on the fringe of the sticks to quietly get himself stoned. He felt that there were times when a man was entitled to do this and for Harry Starky the second of June was the day he took his entitlement. It was also Harry Starky's fortieth birthday. A day when he had every right to get himself high. To look at himself – to see how he was faring.

He looked again into the mirror. It wasn't a bad face, he thought. At least not bad for forty. It had matured reasonably well. Nothing striking about it, but pleasant enough. Perhaps his cheeks had fattened out too much, but his eyes were still an attractive brown, and he still had his own teeth and

17

hair, although his hair was getting thinner and receding a little too quickly, he thought. In fact if he was being honest with himself he would have admitted that it troubled him. But he wasn't. Hell, on the whole, not bad, he thought. It wouldn't win any beauty prize, but then it never had. No, he was satisfied with what he saw, and as for his figure – well, again it was average. Slightly overweight, but not too much fat about. He could hold his own. There was that blonde in the typing pool at the plant who was always giving him the green light – and Mrs Bradley. There was always Mrs Bradley. She had hidden passions. And there was Mary. Yes, he thought, there was Mary. She was a nice kid. Damned lucky to have her around. He frowned and studied his glass.

Suddenly he felt deflated and momentarily frightened. He was forty, single, and in a bar in skids row getting drunk. God! what a life. He took another drink – a long, stiff one. What a life, he thought. He pulled himself together. Perhaps at forty-one, things would be different.

'Yeah,' he grunted aloud. 'They'll be different.'

He looked around the bar to see if his remark had disturbed anyone. He needn't have bothered. The bar attendant had his ears pinned to a radio set, and the only other occupants were two couples both with their minds set on other things than Harry Starky. One of the couples looked like college kids. The girl giggled at every remark her boy friend made. They had sat on the same drink for about an hour. The other couple would probably end up doing the same thing as the college kids, but their approach was more business-like. She was one of the broads from Ma Hollings' place. The man with her was probably an out of town executive – over-weight, over fifty and over-anxious. He was plying her with drinks. He needn't have bothered. The green backs were all she was after. If he wasn't careful he would end up under the table and not in her bed.

Starky poured another drink and tidied up the mess on his table, wiping the cigarette ash into the ash tray. Living alone he had developed neat, tidy habits. The college kid put a nickel in the juke box and the room suddenly re-echoed to a loud jumble of noise representing a form of modern music. The bar attendant scowled openly and put his ear closer to his radio. Starky poured himself three fingers, sank it, and felt sorry for himself. Sorry because, despite his job at the plant, and his executive bungalow, he was forty and he was lonely. Would anybody, anywhere, he wondered, be interested to know that it was his fortieth birthday and he was lonely? Mary? Would she? Perhaps, he thought. He didn't really know about her. And he wasn't really thinking about Mary.

Gradually the effect of the liquor began to ease the pain and allowed his thoughts to look on the brighter side. On the face of it you're doing O.K. Harry, he said to himself. No ailments. A1 at the last physical. What more do you want? A dame? Again he grunted aloud. Did he really want a dame? A companion? He considered the point. Perhaps he did, he thought. Perhaps that was what was troubling him. Perhaps he wanted to belong again. But he knew there was something else. Something he didn't want to think about.

The music stopped and the record returned to its place in the juke box. The silence was golden. Starky heard the bartender and the college kid having a few words. When he looked up he saw the kid had collected his girl friend and was leaving. The bartender had returned to his radio. Starky looked at the bottle. It was half gone. He poured some more drink into his glass and found his hand was unsteady. Ho! Ho! he chuckled. You are on your way, Harry boy. On your way. He lit a cigarette and inhaled the smoke. His last drink had killed all the pain. He sat facing the bottle, a fixed grin on his face. He didn't hear the juke box start up again, or if he did it didn't appear to register with him. Nor did the laughter and shouts that came from the next cubicle, or the arguments. When the bartender ventured solo from the bar to clear the ashtrays, he got the impression that Starky was in his own little world. There was a far away look in Starky's eyes.

When Starky finally decided it was time to go home, he struggled to his feet and in a manner befitting his quota of liquor, staggered to the entrance door. Nobody worried about him, as nobody was there except the bartender who had previously collected more than his correct amount of dollars from Starky, and was checking his till.

The warm night air didn't make Starky feel any better, but the realisation that he was no longer in the seclusion of the bar made him steady himself. He stood for a moment inhaling the air, strongly perfumed by the paper mill, and then headed towards the centre of the town.

'Cab?'

Starky stopped in his tracks and swayed.

'You want to go somewhere?' a voice asked – an Irish voice.

Starky saw a head looking at him through the window of a car. If he had looked closer, he might have noticed that it wasn't one of the regular town cabs.

'Yeah,' Starky said. His voice sounded unfamiliar and distant, his words slurred. 'Riverside Estate. Bungalow No. 7.'

'Get in.'

Starky fell into the back seat. The door closed as if by magic and he felt himself being transported away from the place of his intoxication.

The cab driver began to hum a tune. Starky recognised it. 'I'll take you home again Kathleen,' he mused. Not really an Irish tune.

'You work at the plant?' The cab driver's soft Irish brogue drifted across to Starky.

'Yeah.'

'Heard they make good dough there.'

'Yeah.'

Starky felt incapable of saying anything else.

The cab driver got the message. He returned to his humming. Starky sat without consciously thinking of anything. He saw the city lights as they passed through the High Street and on to the highway.

'What number did you say?' the cab driver asked.

'Seven,' Starky replied and hiccupped. 'It's the first one.'

'Like it up there?'

'Yeah.'

Starky closed his eyes. Like it up there? Where the hell did he think it was? It was only twenty minutes from the town. Seven bungalows tucked away on a piece of land close to the river. Riverside Estate, or the Isolation Unit, as it was called by the workers at the plant. It had been developed as a private estate, but the plant had taken it over for their executive staff, only to find that their executive staff had other ideas. They preferred to live on the Hill Park Estate next to the golf course and Country Club. So Riverside had been handed over to the Research Unit to house their key men. Seven bungalows and seven key men. Three scientists, the Director, Mrs Bradley the Administrative Officer, McIntyre, the plant Security Officer, and Starky. A nice little group. Starky grinned. The Director tried hard to make them into a close-knit circle, but it was under sufferance. They all would have preferred to have got away from the plant altogether. At Riverside it never left them. McIntyre brought his security home with him, the Director brought the plant, and the scientists brought their work. Only Starky and Mrs Bradley tried to leave the plant behind. Mrs Bradley by being active in the town. Starky by doing anything – including getting drunk!

'This is it?'

Starky peered out of the window.

'Yeah. How much?'

'Five bucks.'

Starky paid the cab driver.

'You O.K.?' the man asked.

'Sure.'

Starky got out of the cab. The cab driver swung around and drove off. Starky stood at the foot of his driveway. He saw the lights of Mrs Bradley's bungalow and the McIntyres', but the rest of the estate was in darkness. He wondered what Mrs Bradley would think of him if she saw him now. He gave a chuckle. Probably wish she had joined him. He suspected that she was a secret drinker. He swayed slightly and walked very slowly up the path to the entrance door. He fumbled in his pocket for his house key, found it, and tried to insert it in the lock. The door responded without the key releasing the lock. Starky watched it move. When it was fully ajar, he saw the light shining from under his bedroom door.

'What the hell?' he muttered. 'Anyone there?' he called out, his voice sounding distant and strange. There came no reply. 'Ah! Hell,' he said aloud. He closed the door behind him and crossed the entrance hall, making a parabolic curve to the bedroom door. Leaning heavily against the door surround, he pushed open the door. The room was brightly lit. He focused his eyes at the bouncing objects.

Gradually they settled down. There was something on his bed. It was a figure! A nude figure! 'Oh! no,' he groaned. 'Oh, no.' He screwed his eyes into their sockets. The figure on the bed took shape. It was the naked body of a woman lying face upwards! She was spread-eagled on the bed in such a pose that it made him want to throw up. 'Oh, no,' he groaned again.

He closed his eyes, grimaced, and fought off the urge to be sick. His knees felt weak. His body sagged. He opened his eyes and forced himself forward and stood over the body. It was Laura Nolan, a secretary in the

Research Centre. Her eyes and mouth were wide open. There was a red weal around her neck. She was dead.

Suddenly the urge to throw up became uncontrollable.

THREE

Lieutenant Hugan drank his coffee and gritted his teeth. He was standing at the window, his back to the four shirt-sleeved detectives who were seated at the table. It was hot in the room, and the air was filled with cigarette smoke. Lieutenant Hugan was in a bad mood. He always was these days. The rest of the room waited for his sharp, caustic orders. They admired his thoroughness and ability. They didn't like his manner and attitude. Neither did Hugan. Why the hell did a homicide investigation always have to start in the middle of the night? he wondered. Why couldn't it be at some civilised time of the day? He could just picture Madge's reactions. She was becoming more difficult each day. This was more fuel for her fire. She had never really been a policeman's wife. Now it was worse. Always nagging at him to retire so that they could get away. God! did she want him to be put out to graze already? The thought rankled him. He liked the Force. He liked being in charge of a homicide squad, but the more he worked at it the worse it became with Madge. Again he scowled and threw his paper cup into the basket. He swung around and looked at the four faces turned in his direction. He had a lean, scraggy face which looked as if it had been roughed up a few times. His hair was grey, short and strong. His body was like his face.

The door opened and a burly, plain-clothed detective sergeant, Sergeant Shean, came into the room. He wiped the perspiration from his brow and sighed.

'Starky keep to his story?' Hugan asked crisply.

'Yeah,' the sergeant agreed. 'Couldn't budge him.'

Hugan walked over to the door, opened it and looked at the bent figure of Starky leaning against the desk. He saw an over-weight figure with an all-round image of a man about to go to seed. There was something pathetic about Starky. His neck tie was loose, his shirt open. He looked tired and beaten. Hugan closed the door.

'Let him go,' he snapped. 'You got his statement?'

'Yes, boss.'

Hugan moved his head. The sergeant left

the room. Hugan went and sat at the head of the table.

'Let's go over the details again,' he said when the sergeant had rejoined them. 'Let's start with the girl.'

One of the detectives opened his notebook.

'Name, Laura Nolan,' he said. 'Age twenty-three. Worked as a secretary to the special research unit at the plant. A Government project.'

Government! Government! Hugan inwardly cursed. They were going to have to contend with Washington breathing down their necks in addition to everything else.

'Was born in Ainsworth, a small town in Nebraska. She had an apartment at No. 175 West Street. Last night she returned to her apartment round about eighteen hundred hours, got changed and went out.'

'Her own car?'

'Yes, a 1970 Ford Convertible. That was the last she was seen.'

'The car?'

'We sent out a call. Half an hour ago a patrolman found it at the Country Club.'

'Country Club,' Hugan muttered.

'Laski is at present searching her rooms,' the detective continued.

Hugan grunted his agreement. 'What about Starky?' he asked.

Sergeant Shean picked up a sheet of paper. 'In your own words,' the lieutenant ordered. He lit another cigarette and threw away the empty packet. His mouth felt rough. He wished he could give the damned things up.

'Harry Starky, aged 40 years,' the sergeant said in his broad New York accent which was a legacy from his youth. 'Born in Philadelphia. His folks were naturalised Poles. Formerly called Sterenonski. They came to the States in 1910. Changed their name to Starky in 1916. Starky graduated from the local High School. Took a course in Business Studies at the Philadelphia Business Institute. Graduated as an accountant. Drifted about a bit. Went over to Europe. Spent a lot of time in the U.K. Married a girl from the Polish community in London in 1959. Had a baby daughter in 62. The marriage folded up. His wife left him and went back to Poland. She got a divorce in 64. Starky returned to the States in 66. Got a job in Chicago, then moved to Pittsburg. Last year he was appointed to his present position as Accounting Officer to the Research Project at A.C.I. – a Government appointment.'

Hugan looked pensive. He didn't know why, but Starky bugged him and he didn't like it. He sat deep in thought, trying to analyse his doubts, his scraggy face looking like a piece of rock hewn out of a quarry. Was it because Starky had stuck so rigidly to his story despite all the liquor he had drunk? Hugan wondered. Or was it because he had sobered up too quickly? There was something that had got under the lieutenant's skin. Across the road a clock chimed giving the time as seven a.m. It stirred the lieutenant into action.

'Hank,' he said to the sergeant. 'Get on to Philadelphia police. Send them a photograph over the wire. Have Starky's background checked out. He bugs me.'

'O.K., Lieutenant,' Shean said.

'And check his alibi,' the lieutenant added. He turned to the other detectives. 'Lew, check Laura Nolan's background. I want a full dossier on her. I want to know what she was wearing on the night of her murder – everything about her. Joe, you get out to the Club. Search the grounds. Luke, you come with me to the plant.'

There was a knock on the door.

'Come in,' the lieutenant shouted. A uniformed policeman entered and handed the lieutenant a folder. The lieutenant opened it and read its contents.

'The pathologist's report,' he said to the assembled group. 'Laura Nolan died of asphyxiation caused by strangulation. Time of death is confirmed at approximately between 20.00 and 20.30 hours. She was not pregnant and had not been sexually attacked.'

'Then why strip her naked?' somebody asked.

'Perhaps somebody wanted to mislead us,' the lieutenant said grimly. 'Report back here tonight at 18.00 hours.' Madge wasn't going to like that, he thought. He scowled and looked grim. The detectives took it as a sign that he was getting steamed up about the case and hurriedly set about their business. The lieutenant remained seated for a while and wondered how the people at the plant were going to react to the murder.

The news of the murder shook Medway Springs as well as the employees of the A.C.I. Plant. Medway Springs was a small town tucked away amongst the lakes of Northern Minnesota. A local murder always made headlines in the town's newspaper.

The staff of the Research Centre took a while to get over their initial shock. They gathered in small groups and fully digested what gossip, or inference, could be gleaned from the newspaper, or what was known not only about the victim, but also Harry Starky who had suddenly become the central figure in the case. Work in the department was non-existent for the first two hours.

The people with whom Laura Nolan had had the closest contact reacted differently to the news. Dr Logan, the Research Director, was deeply distressed, more so than he displayed. Dr Kay, the British scientist, was sullen and uncommunicative. Dr Ludvick appeared unconcerned. Dr Cusack was sad and kept shaking his head. Benson, Cusack's assistant, put on an air of 'I'm not surprised'. McIntyre, the Security Officer, was worried. Anything affecting the project security affected him and this was a major issue. Mrs Bradley, the Administrative Officer, took the news phlegmatically. She had never been one of Laura Nolan's admirers.

When Dr Logan arrived at the plant, he refused to speak to the two reporters who had been patiently waiting for the refusal, although he had no objection to having his photograph taken. After a hasty examination of his mail he put through a call to Washington and assured Senator Leebright that nothing would interfere with their deadline, and that he would personally guarantee that the report would be ready for him on schedule. A promise which he hoped he could fulfil, as the Senator had left him in no doubt of the outcome if anything misfired. Logan didn't want to fall foul of the Senator, or Washington, at this late stage. Within a few weeks he could be free of them with a clean slate. Medway Springs was going to be his spring board. Blast Laura Nolan! he thought. If he wasn't careful her murder could upset his plans. Blast her.

After speaking to Washington, Logan held a brief conversation with the Managing Director of the plant. When he had finished, his secretary, Mary Lewis, told him that Lieutenant Hugan of Homicide and another detective were waiting to see him. Logan gave a resigned sigh and prepared to meet them.

The two detectives were shown into the room. Logan thought how grim and sour they looked. Not as glamorised as on the T.V. shows. Lieutenant Hugan, in turn, saw a suave, six-foot man in his late forties. A well educated man with an executive air about him, and a handsome face which looked as if it had been well taken care of.

'I am Lieutenant Hugan of Homicide,' Hugan grunted. 'This is Detective Beaumont.'

'Sit down, gentlemen,' Logan said.

The two detectives sat down.

'You have read the morning paper?' Hugan asked.

'Yes,' Logan sighed. 'Nasty business.'

'Would you mind telling me about her?'

'Well, I can't really say very much,' Logan said guardedly. 'She was employed as a secretary by my unit and seconded to the special research project so that her services were more or less used by the research team.'

'Who engaged her?' Hugan asked.

'Well, I did,' Logan replied. 'On Mrs Bradley's advice. She is my Administrative Officer.'

The detective made note of the name.

'And she worked exclusively for these – how many scientists are there?'

'Four altogether.'

'Was she a popular girl?'

'I believe so. I never received any complaints about her.'

'I understand you use the Country Club,' Hugan said.

'Yes, that is correct. Mostly at weekends.'

'Have you ever seen Miss Nolan there?'

'Yes. She has been there.'

'With whom?'

Logan looked pensive.

'Various people.'

'Who?' Hugan sighed impatiently.

'Well, she has been there with Mr Starky,' Logan said quietly, 'and Dr Kay, one of the scientists.'

'Anyone else?'

'There was somebody from town once and a chemist from the plant.'

'She got about,' Beaumont remarked dryly.

'She wasn't unattractive,' Logan replied evenly.

'You ever take her out?' Hugan snapped and was quick to see Logan flush up.

'No,' Logan retorted hesitantly, but Hugan didn't believe him.

'Do you mind if we ask about?' Hugan asked. 'Talk to the people she worked with?'

'You'll have to see McIntyre.'

'McIntyre?'

'He is responsible for all security. His office is across the parking lot in the research station. You'll have to co-operate with him.'

'A Government man or plant?'

'Government. The Senate Committee

appointed him.'

'Senate Committee?' Hugan asked suspiciously. 'Who is in charge of this Centre?'

'It's a Government project,' Logan explained. 'Senator Leebright is head of the Committee.'

'Senator Leebright,' Hugan growled. He knew the man. Everyone in the State knew the Senator. The lieutenant openly scowled his displeasure.

'Is this research top security?' he asked.

Logan hesitated and then said 'Yes.'

Hugan grunted. His feeling about the case was beginning to prove itself correct. There were going to be barriers and walls put up in front of him.

'I'll see McIntyre. What about Mrs Bradley?'

'She's in this building. My secretary will get her for you.' Logan moved towards his intercom.

'That's O.K.,' the lieutenant said. 'I'll ask her on the way out.'

The two detectives moved to the door, but before leaving the room, the lieutenant turned to Logan.

'How do you rate Starky?' he asked quietly.

'Oh! a good man,' Logan replied cautiously. 'A bit unimaginative. Very neat, tidy sort of worker. The solid, steady type.'

'Hm,' Hugan grunted. 'Was his appointment a Government one?'

'Yes,' Logan replied. 'On my recommendation, of course.'

'Of course. Thanks.'

The two detectives left the room. Mary Lewis looked up from her typewriter and smiled at them. She had a friendly smile which lit up her face. Hugan stopped and allowed his granite features to give an apology of a smile. He liked the look of the girl. She was like the kid next door – everyone's kid next door. Not an outstanding good looker, but a nice pleasant face to have around. And her hair was neat and tidy. She looked as if she also had a trim figure. Probably the type that was always cheerful, Hugan thought. There weren't many of them about. Madge had been like that once, but not any longer.

'Where do I find Mrs Bradley?' he asked.

'First on the right down the corridor,' Mary Lewis replied. She had a slight catch in her voice – a pleasant catch.

'Thanks,' Hugan replied. 'By the way, what was Laura Nolan like?'

Mary smiled. 'Well, I suppose that depends.'

'On what?'

'Whether you are a man or a woman.'

'How?'

'Well, all the men seemed to find her attractive. She dressed well and was easy to get on with.' She dropped her eyes.

Easy to get into bed with? Hugan wondered.

'And the women?'

'She didn't seem to have much time for us females,' Mary added. 'It's a pity, but I never really got to know her. She was efficient with her work. Very good at it.'

A man's woman, Hugan thought. He wasn't surprised.

'Which is Mr Starky's room?' he asked.

He saw Mary blush up and wondered what the link was. She seemed too nice a kid for Starky.

'His room is directly opposite,' she said and turned her head away.

'Thank you.'

Mary continued with her typing. Hugan and Beaumont left the room.

'Well, that's two extra bits of information,' Hugan growled. 'The Director has probably been dating Laura Nolan and his secretary is carrying a torch for Starky.'

'I think the Director hasn't been the only

one Laura Nolan has entertained,' Beaumont said.

'That, I think, is an understatement. Come on, let's talk to Mrs Bradley and see what picture she gives of her.'

Mrs Bradley's picture was very similar to Mary's.

'She was efficient which is what matters,' she said in reply to the lieutenant's question.

'Did you like her?'

Mrs Bradley removed her spectacles and looked at the lieutenant coldly. She was a woman the wrong side of forty. A big woman, well made, but evenly proportioned. Her hair was grey and tinted. Her features sagging and heavily made up – a bit too heavily made up, Hugan thought. He looked into her eyes. There was a trace of redness about them. They had a mushy look. Not as clear and decisive as Mrs Bradley's manner implied.

'Is that relevant?' she asked icily.

'I think so or I would not have asked,' the lieutenant replied equally unfriendly.

'I didn't like her,' Mrs Bradley said. 'She seemed too interested in other people.'

'Such as?'

'Men, Lieutenant, men.'

'And in particular?' the lieutenant insisted.

'That I don't know,' Mrs Bradley said defiantly. 'She appeared to like them all.'

'Mr Starky, for instance?'

'I would imagine so,' Mrs Bradley snapped.

'Dr Logan?'

Mrs Bradley flushed up.

'Dr Kay? Dr Ludvick?' the lieutenant added.

'I don't know,' Mrs Bradley said.

'You engaged Laura Nolan,' the lieutenant said, rushing her. 'What was her background?'

'Came from a small town,' Mrs Bradley replied slowly and calmly. 'Somewhere in Nebraska. Did a secretarial course. She then went to Chicago. Had a couple of jobs there. Both large industrial concerns.'

'Good references?'

'Excellent, and she was very efficient.'

'So everyone keeps telling me,' Hugan sighed. 'You got her records.'

'Yes,' Mrs Bradley replied.

'Let me see them.'

Mrs Bradley looked as if she was going to refuse.

'Come on, come on,' Hugan snapped. 'Do you want me to issue a warrant or something?'

Mrs Bradley silently showed her displeasure. She went to a filing cabinet.

'And Starky's,' Hugan added.

'Well, I'm not sure…'

'Look, Mrs Bradley. I haven't got all day.' Hugan was becoming irritated with her attitude.

Mrs Bradley produced two folders. She handed them to the lieutenant. He gave one to his assistant and studied the remainder. It was Starky's particulars. He glanced at the facts. One piece of information made him raise his eyebrows.

When he was through he closed the folder. He looked across at Beaumont to exchange files, but his assistant was still studying the contents of his folder. The lieutenant glanced at Mrs Bradley and was surprised to see that she was also watching Beaumont. And there was something in the way that she was looking at him that made the lieutenant frown. It was almost as if she was mentally stripping him. The lieutenant looked at his assistant. He was young, athletic, virile. Was the Bradley dame attracted physically? he wondered. Was his interpretation of the look correct? Beaumont felt the lieutenant's eyes on him. He looked up. Mrs Bradley looked away. The look on her face changed. The lieutenant exchanged folders with his assistant and made a mental note of what he had seen.

'I might want a photostat of these,' he said when he was through with the two dossiers.

'Will there be anything else?' Mrs Bradley asked coolly, ignoring the lieutenant's remark.

'Did you hear a car drive up to Mr Starky's bungalow last night?'

Mrs Bradley frowned.

'No,' she replied. 'I have already told one of your detectives. I was playing my tape recorder. I didn't hear anything.'

'But you heard Mr Starky return about eleven?'

'I didn't hear or see anything,' Mrs Bradley added firmly.

'What time did you leave the plant last night?'

'Six p.m.'

'Go straight to your bungalow?'

'No. I went into town and picked up a costume.'

'Costume?' Hugan asked. 'From which store?'

'Not a store, Lieutenant. It was a theatrical costume. I am rehearsing a musical play at the High School.'

'Where did you collect this costume?' Hugan persisted.

'From a member of the cast.'

'Name and address?' Hugan snapped.

'Mr Leopold, 65 Vine Street,' Mrs Bradley sighed.

'What time?'

'About six-fifteen.'

Hugan looked at Beaumont and saw that he had noted the facts.

'And then you went direct to your bungalow?' Hugan asked.

'No, I went to the rehearsal.'

'At the High School.'

'Yes.'

'What time did you leave?'

'About nine o'clock. I got home about nine-twenty.'

'The rest of the cast leave then?'

'I don't know, Lieutenant,' Mrs Bradley sighed, 'you will have to ask them.'

'I will,' Hugan snapped. 'Thank you for being so helpful,' he added. 'We will probably be back.'

'Goodbye, Lieutenant.'

When they were in the corridor, the lieutenant turned to his assistant.

'What do you make of her?'

'An aggressive spinster,' Beaumont said.

'Yeah,' Hugan agreed, but wondered if there was also another side to her.

'What about the records?' Beaumont asked.

'Nothing we didn't know,' Hugan growled, 'except that Starky dropped money to take up his present appointment.'

'Not usual.'

'No,' Hugan agreed. 'Perhaps his guy McIntyre might tell us what is so special about this place and its crew.'

But McIntyre wasn't forthcoming. He was a tough, red-haired Scot who had Senator Leebright and Washington looking over his shoulder. The security of the research project was McIntyre's responsibility. In a week's time the project would be off his hands. Until then he didn't want anything to interfere with its final stages. And that included Lieutenant Hugan and Laura Nolan's murder. Hugan immediately sensed McIntyre's feelings and an atmosphere developed between the two men. Hugan dug in his toes and persisted, but he got little out of McIntyre. In McIntyre's eyes Laura Nolan had been attractive, sexy, but frigid. She had worked well and caused no bother. Other than that McIntyre couldn't help, or as the lieutenant suspected –

wouldn't help.

'What were your movements last night?' Hugan asked sharply.

'I was at the plant all evening up till about 10 p.m.,' McIntyre replied.

'Can you verify that?'

McIntyre shrugged. 'Ask the guards. Some of them saw me.'

'I will,' Hugan growled. 'Now I would like to meet your precious chicks. That is, if you don't mind.'

McIntyre did mind and it showed, but he knew he couldn't buck the lieutenant any further. He brought the four scientists to his room and introduced them to the lieutenant. Cusack was small, elderly, with grey balding hair and a stooped gait. He kept shaking his head and muttering about the tragedy of Laura Nolan's death, but he couldn't offer any help. In his eyes Laura Nolan had been a nice, quiet girl, and an efficient secretary. The previous evening he had returned to his bungalow with Dr Ludvick and had not left it all evening. He had not seen, or heard, anything.

Ludvick was tall, erect and serious-faced. He was Cusack's chief assistant. To him Laura Nolan had been someone who had done the necessary secretarial work. Otherwise she need never have existed. The previous evening after returning to the Riverside Estate with Dr Cusack he had remained in his bungalow all evening with his wife. He had also not seen, or heard, anything that would help the lieutenant.

Kay was a little more informative. Younger than Ludvick, he was a polished, well groomed, bachelor. He admitted having dated Laura Nolan a couple of times, but flushed up at Hugan's suggestion that he had had an affair with her. They had been friendly and that was all. The previous evening Kay had gone direct to the Country Club where he had spent the evening. Helen Logan had also been at the Club playing bridge and would verify his whereabouts. Hugan managed to make Kay flush up again by asking if his meetings with Helen Logan had been accidental or arranged.

Warren Benson, the youngest of the group, was a former student of Dr Cusack's at Columbia University. He was the odd one out in his style of dress and appearance which still identified him with his student days. To him Laura Nolan had been a mixed up chick. An intelligent, well-read kid, who had lacked purpose. Lately he had thought she had appeared worried and quiet, but she had refused to talk to Benson about it. Benson had been friendly with her, but although they roomed close to each other, they had never dated. The previous evening Benson had returned to his apartment and spent the evening reading.

Hugan cross examined them all closely and at length, but when he and Beaumont later drove back to the station he admitted that Laura Nolan had him puzzled.

'According to the guards she was a sex bird,' Beaumont said, 'but there was no tie up with anyone in particular.'

'They all gave a different picture of the girl,' Hugan growled. 'And nobody heard or saw anything last night.' He scowled and gritted his teeth. 'You would think that at least one of them on that blasted estate would have seen or heard something.'

He glowered and stared out of the window. It was going to be a long, rough, stinking case, he thought. Before it was through he would either be finished with the Force or Madge would be finished with him.

At the station, Sergeant Shean gave him another problem.

'Starky's alibi is wide open, Lieutenant,' he said.

'Spell it out, Hank,' Hugan snapped.

'The bar attendant at Luigi's saloon was on a one night stand. A drifter. He took off this morning for Chicago.'

The lieutenant snorted like a wounded lion.

'There are no Irish singing cab drivers – or even Irish cabbies. And none of the cab companies reckon they operate from the area of Luigi's saloon.'

'You been around the lot?'

'Yeah, every one of them.'

'What about Starky's car?'

'It was parked in the lot at the rear of the Central Garage as he said. It needs a couple of new brake linings.'

'The night attendant see it arrive?'

'No, but it could have been left there while he was having his supper, between seven-thirty and eight.'

'So no one sees Starky park his car,' Hugan said thoughtfully. 'No one can substantiate his alibi in the bar, and there is no cab driver to say he took him home.'

'That's it, boss. Straight along the line.'

The lieutenant looked pensive. Starky had bugged him from the beginning. He bugged him even more now. With what the sergeant had told him, he could make Starky sweat. He could even pin the rap on him.

'Do we bring him in for questioning?' the sergeant asked.

'Not yet,' Hugan replied grimly. 'Let's wait until Philadelphia have run the rule over him. Then we'll bring him in.'

Things were beginning to hot up, Hugan thought. There was a chink in the darkness.

'Your wife phoned when you were out. Wants you to call her.'

'Thanks,' Hugan growled and inwardly cursed. He didn't like Madge phoning him at work. Not when he was working on a case. Why the hell couldn't she have waited until he got home?

'Anything else?' he asked.

'Yeah,' the sergeant replied in a voice that meant he had saved the worst to the last. 'The chief wants to see you as soon as you're free.'

'That'll be never,' Hugan growled and decided to get it off his list first.

He went up to the chief's office and entered the room. The Chief of Police looked up from behind his mahogany desk.

'Ah! John,' he said. 'Come and sit down.'

The chief sat back in his chair.

'How are your investigations going?' he asked.

'It's early days,' Hugan said, 'but this case

has a sour taste about it.'

'Hm.' The chief toyed with a pencil. There was a serious look on his face. Hugan wondered what the hell it was leading up to.

'I want you to play this one careful, John,' the chief said guardedly. 'No leaning on anyone. Nothing unorthodox.'

Hugan jumped to his feet. 'Hell! Chief!' he exploded. 'What am I supposed to do? Wear kid gloves?'

'Sit down, John,' the chief said forcibly. 'Sit down.'

Hugan sat down.

'I don't want to tie your hands,' the chief continued. 'I just want you to play it strictly according to the book. No short cuts. No premature arrests. Don't hold anyone unless it will stick.'

Hugan gritted his teeth.

'What gives, Chief?' he asked grimly.

The chief looked equally grim.

'Let's just say that I have been tipped off,' he said. 'For some reason a certain Senator has this town in his sights. Get it?'

'Got it,' Hugan replied flatly.

The two men looked at each other. Hugan wondered why the chief didn't spell it out fully. That Laura Nolan had been on the staff of a research unit lorded over by Senator

Leebright. That the Senator was ready to take the town apart if it suited his book.

The chief placed a pencil back on its stand. The interview was over.

'Keep me posted,' he said.

'Sure, chief.'

Hugan returned to his own room. So Leebright had his sights on Medway Springs, he thought. Well, Hugan was going to carry out the investigation as he thought fit. To hell with Leebright. He called Sergeant Shean into his room.

'We'll bring Starky in,' he said. 'I want to hear what he has to say for himself.'

'Yes, sir,' Shean said enthusiastically. 'Straight away?'

'No,' Hugan replied. 'We'll wait until he leaves the plant.'

'O.K. boss – anything else?'

'Yes,' Hugan said thoughtfully. 'I want to know all about that crew at the plant. Dig into their past and dig deep. Make it priority. I want the information quickly. We might not be able to find out why the hell they are so important as to warrant a full time nursemaid, but at least we can find out what makes them tick.'

A deep frown appeared on the lieutenant's face. Sergeant Shean saw it and tactfully withdrew. He knew the lieutenant was building himself up into a filthy mood. He wondered what was griping him. The chief? His wife? Or Starky? Starky! Harry Starky, the sergeant mused. Some birthday present! Wonder how he made out today?

Harry Starky spent the first day of his forty-first year looking as if the cares of the world were on his shoulders. He looked lousy. He hadn't had much sleep and it showed. When he eventually arrived at the Research Centre, he found a note on his desk telling him that Dr Logan wanted to see him. He rang his secretary and asked her to bring him a cup of black coffee. When she brought it she looked at him as if he was some form of monster with two heads. It was the same when he went to see the Director. He had to collect some papers from the general office and his presence brought about an immediate lull in the general undertone of conversation and movement. They eyed him with curiosity and there was a quick exchange of knowing glances around the room. Logan acted coolly. He gave Starky only a half-hearted form of encouragement and pressed him into getting out the estimates for the next project. Only Mary Lewis showed that she thought he was not some form of bluebeard.

'Oh! Harry,' she said with feeling, when he entered her room. 'How awful for you.' Her face reflected her genuine concern.

Starky grimaced and adjusted his necktie.

'What a bloody business,' he said. 'Why would anyone want to murder Laura Nolan? And why dump her body in my bungalow?'

'Perhaps they knew that you were out,' Mary said without realising the significance of her remark.

Starky looked at her thoughtfully.

'I had never thought of it that way, Mary,' he said.

'Well, I'm sure the police will solve it very soon,' Mary said encouragingly. 'The lieutenant has been here.'

'Don't mention the police to me,' Starky said. 'I've spent the night with them.'

'You do look tired, Harry,' Mary said gently. 'Do you want to call it off tonight?'

'Tonight?' Starky asked, and then remembered he had promised to go to Jayson Hendrich's party. Hell! he thought, was Jayson still giving his party? It seemed a little indecent. They had all known Laura, including Jayson.

'Is Jayson still giving his party?' he asked. 'Surely he could have put it off.'

'Not Jayson,' Mary sighed. 'If he's giving a party nothing is going to stop him.' She looked at him with her large, blue eyes. 'I suppose it is no good moping about it, Harry. Life has to go on.'

'True!' Starky sighed.

'Then you will come?'

'Oh! I don't know, Mary,' he said. 'Everyone seems to think that I'm some sort of freak.'

'Well I don't and neither does Jayson. He phoned earlier and asked me to tell you that he expects you to be there.'

'O.K. Mary, I'll give it a try.'

Starky returned to his office and tried to bury himself in his work, but his mind kept turning to the dead body of Laura Nolan on his bed. At six p.m. he collected Mary and together they left the office. Outside on the roadway was a yellow and black police car. Inside was one of the detectives Starky had seen the previous evening. Mary saw Starky hesitate and caught an anxious look on his face.

'They aren't waiting for you,' she said sweetly.

But they were.

As they descended the flight of steps the car door opened and a detective got out. He raised his hat apologetically.

'Mr Starky,' he said. 'Would you mind coming down to the station?'

'What for?' Starky snapped. 'I have told you everything.'

'The lieutenant would like to ask you a few more questions.'

The detective opened the rear door. Starky knew that he had no alternative. He turned to Mary.

'Do you want me to come with you, Harry?' Mary asked anxiously.

'No, Mary. This won't take long.'

'Shall I pick you up?'

'No, I'll take a cab to Jayson's house. I'll see you there.'

'All right.'

Starky got into the police car. The detective got in beside him. As they drove away Starky saw several faces turned in their direction. He shrank into the corner of the car.

At the station he was taken into a room and confronted by Lieutenant Hugan and Sergeant Shean. It was stifling hot in the room. The two police officers were shirt-sleeved, the sergeant's neck tie was unfastened. Starky could feel the perspiration start to roll down his face.

'Mr Starky,' the lieutenant said, with very

little movement of his lips, 'tell us again, in detail, what you did last night between the hours of 6 p.m. and finding Laura Nolan's body in your bungalow.'

There was something in the lieutenant's dull monotone that sounded ominous.

'I left the plant round about six-thirty,' Starky said hesitantly.

'Exactly?' the sergeant growled.

'About a couple of minutes after,' Starky replied, and wiped his brow. 'I went to my bungalow.'

'How long did it take you?'

'About twenty minutes,' Starky said.

'What then?'

'Had a shower, got changed.'

'What time did you leave?'

'About seven-thirty.'

'Go on.'

Again Starky wiped the perspiration from his brow.

'I drove into town, left my car in the parking lot at the rear of the Central Garage, and walked to Luigi's.'

'Walked?'

'It's only a few blocks,' Starky explained.

'What about the attendant at the garage? Did he see you?'

'I don't know,' Starky replied nervously. 'I

had phoned them in the afternoon and arranged to leave the car.'

'Did you see anybody at the parking lot?'

'No,' Starky said and frowned.

'Go on.'

'I walked to Luigi's saloon,' Starky said again.

'Why did you pick Luigi's saloon?' Sergeant Shean asked, towering over Starky.

'I don't really know,' Starky mumbled.

'Speak up.'

'I don't really know. I have had a drink there before and it has been quiet. I thought it would be a good place to have a drink without being bothered. I just wanted to be alone.'

'Alone! Who was in there?'

'Only the bartender when I arrived.'

'Describe him,' the sergeant bellowed.

'Medium height,' Starky said. 'Dark, well greased hair. Pointed features. Slightly overweight I would say. Age round about forty-five.'

The two police officers exchanged glances.

'Look, what's this all about?' Starky asked. 'I've told you all this before.'

'So he has,' the sergeant sneered.

Again the two police officers exchanged glances.

'Tell him,' Hugan said gruffly.

The sergeant placed his body on the table in front of Starky.

'We checked your story, Mr Starky,' he said in a tone which mixed derision with sadistic pleasure. 'It doesn't hold water.'

'What do you mean?' Starky asked hotly. 'I told you the truth.' He stood up.

'Sit down!' the lieutenant snapped.

Starky sat down.

'The bartender was not as you described him,' the sergeant continued more evenly. 'He was a man called Joseph Patteneli. He was five foot eight inches in height, slim and bald. His age was fifty-six.'

'No!' Starky exclaimed. 'No!'

'And another thing. There is no cab driver in the town who fits the description you gave us and no company operates a pick up from that area.'

Starky looked at them dumbfounded. 'No cab driver?' he asked.

'No cab driver,' the sergeant sighed. 'So let us get down to details.' He looked stern and unfriendly. 'Detailed descriptions which we can check, or else...'

FOUR

Jayson Hendrich was a big man. Big in build, big at the plant, big at the Church, big in local politics and big with his friends. His large physique was a matter of genetics; his position at the plant, where he was on the Board, was through his own hard work. The remainder of his achievements were through his willingness to spend big. Jayson Hendrich spent money to gather around him the trappings befitting a prosperous, successful man, when he could have achieved similar status symbols with less graft and more honesty, and probably acquired a more sincere collection of friends. People were prepared to accept what Hendrich had to give them, but it was not always a two-way stretch, and the same people were also prepared to run him down behind his back. Starky had got to know him through Mary, and although Starky was a very different character to Hendrich, they had struck up a friendship. Starky was a fair poker player, and being a bachelor was also generally available. This had started the friendship, but what had finally clinched it was their mutual interest in flying. Both Starky and Hendrich held a pilot's licence and they spent a lot of their free time together at Jackson Field. In many ways Starky was one of Hendrich's few true friends. His other friends included the scientists at the plant and a cosmopolitan collection of people who Hendrich felt could further his ambitions. The scientists, Hendrich had cultivated because of their link with Washington and Senator Leebright in particular. Hendrich was just waiting for the day when the backroom boys of the Party were prepared to take him on as their candidate. His sights were set on the next election. Already he had Hank Redman, the Party treasurer, on his side and through the scientists Hendrich hoped to get Senator Leebright's support. When the Senator visited the Research Centre, Hendrich entertained him. Hendrich felt that he had already got to the first base in getting the Senator's support.

The Logans quietly suffered Hendrich without confessing to anyone their true feelings of the man, although Helen Logan occasionally winced at his uncouthness. However, if they suffered Jayson Hendrich they liked his wife, Emily. She, as is often the case, was like chalk to cheese, compared to her husband. Slight in build and over-powered by her husband, she seemed like a mouse with a lion. They had been married for fifteen years, and with no family to knit them together, they lived a fragile, false existence which Hendrich kept together for the respectability he needed. He bullied and rode roughshod over his wife who suffered her indignities in silence.

When Starky finally arrived at Hendrich's house in the Hill Park Estate after his maul-ing with Lieutenant Hugan and Sergeant Shean, the party was in full swing. One thing even Hendrich's critics were all agreed upon, was that he could throw a good party. His plan was simple. Mix them up and give them plenty to drink.

Starky left the cab at the entrance to the driveway. The house was lit up and music carried across the warm, dark night. Starky grimaced. He could hear Hendrich's loud, raucous laughter. He would be beginning to sweat now, Starky thought. He and Hank Redman. They both sweated and kidded themselves that they were the poor gal's Paul Newman. The stupid idiots, Starky thought. They were all stupid. All living a shallow, superficial, aimless existence.

Starky pulled himself up sharply. He didn't have to think like that – it wasn't so. They were a typical, warm hearted cross section of a community, he told himself. He ran his fingers through his hair. The lieutenant had really rattled him. He had to get on top of it again. He just had to.

Starky tried to slip into the party unnoticed, but Hendrich spotted him.

'Hear you been down to the station again, Harry?' he called across above the din of the music. Starky visibly winced. 'Have they got the bum who did it yet?'

'Not yet,' Starky replied. He could feel eyes boring into him. He felt like a naked man. Hendrich came over and slapped him on the shoulder.

'Not to worry, Harry,' he said patronisingly.

'Jayson, I could do with a drink,' Starky said hurriedly before Hendrich said any more. 'Now!' he added.

'Sorry, Harry, help yourself.'

Starky helped himself liberally. The first two he didn't taste, the next two made him feel better.

Mary came over to him. She had been dancing with Hank Redman.

'How did it go, Harry?' she asked anx-

64

iously. She could tell immediately that he had quickly downed a number of drinks and took it to be a bad sign.

'Terrible,' Starky said quietly. He took her by the arm and led her to the open veranda. They were not alone. A small splinter party had formed in the open air and were dancing to a record player. Starky moved away from the dancing.

'Mary,' he said seriously. 'I don't know what the hell is happening.'

She looked at his troubled face and saw the strain.

'Everything I have told them seems to be folding up on me,' he said desperately.

'What do you mean, Harry?'

'No one saw me drop my car off at the Central Garage. The description I gave the police of the bartender doesn't fit with what the police have. No one can be located to confirm that I was actually in the bar, and they can't find the cab driver who took me home.'

'But surely the bartender recognises you, even if your description is different?' Mary said.

'He was a casual,' Starky said sadly. 'He took off this morning.'

'But why have they got a different description of him? Why?' Mary persisted.

'God! I wish I knew,' Harry said. 'And the damned cab driver. He was real enough.'

'Give it time, Harry,' Mary said calmly. 'They are sure to find him. There aren't that many cab drivers in Medway Springs.'

'That's the trouble,' Starky said anxiously. 'The police say they have been around all the cab firms. First, none of them have an Irish cabbie. Secondly, none of them operate from the sticks as a pick up area.'

'But it happened, Harry. It actually happened. It is not part of your imagination.'

'The police are beginning to wonder.'

She put her hand tenderly on his arm.

'It will be all right. You'll see.'

'The trouble is, Mary, I can't give them a lot of details or descriptions.' He looked rueful. 'Not the way I was. I think I'll go back to Luigi's saloon. Something might click.'

'Not tonight, Harry,' Mary said. 'You are too tense. Leave it for a day.'

'Ah! There you are, Mary!' It was Redman again. 'Now, Harry, you can't monopolise her.' His enthusiasm irritated Starky.

'Come on, Mary,' Redman bubbled. 'You did promise me another dance.'

Mary opened her mouth to refuse.

'Go ahead, Mary,' Starky said. He could

do with another drink, he thought.

Redman led Mary away, his face flushed and perspiring. Starky strolled into the library which was being used as a bar. He poured himself a stiff drink.

'Oh! Harry,' a woman's voice said in a stage whisper close to his ear. It was Louella Waterhouse. 'I do hope everything goes all right for you,' she added. 'I'm sure you didn't do it.'

Starky grimaced and stifled a suitable retort.

'Thank you,' he said.

Louella Waterhouse left him with the air of a knight errant who had just performed a good deed. But the damage had been done. When Mary returned from her dance Starky told her that he was leaving.

'I've had enough tonight,' he said.

'I'll drive you home, Harry,' she said.

'Hell, there's no need to, Mary. I can get a cab.'

'I think I'd better,' Mary said gently.

'Thanks.'

They found Hendrich. He was busy pouring his one hundred and seventy pounds over a bottled blonde. They told him that they were leaving.

'See you at the Field, Saturday, Harry,'

Hendrich called out and enveloped the blonde in his bear-like hug.

'They call that dancing,' Harry muttered.

'You'll feel different tomorrow, Harry.'

'Sure.'

They got into Mary's car and drove slowly across town to the Riverside Estate.

'Like to come for a flip, Saturday?' Starky asked.

'Love to, Harry.'

'Good.'

They lapsed into silence. Starky couldn't quite put his finger on his relationship with Mary. He had never got past first base with her. She seemed to treat him more like a brother than a potential lover. But she was a hell of a good kid, he thought. It wasn't with everyone that you could just sit mute and not feel uncomfortable. They came to the small estate.

'Come in for a coffee, Mary.'

'All right, Harry. A quick one.'

She ran the car up to the car port. When Starky got out, he hesitated. It was only twenty-four hours since he had come across Laura Nolan's body. It seemed like a lifetime. He looked across at Mrs Bradley's bungalow and saw the two red squares where the light shone through her curtains. What was she up to in there? he wondered. Knocking back the liquor in her dressing gown? Mary saw him staring across the lawn.

'She'll be listening to her Gilbert and Sullivan,' she said, reading his thoughts.

Starky scowled. 'If she hadn't been listening to her blasted music last night,' he grumbled, 'she would have heard me arrive in the cab.'

They went into the bungalow by the side door. Mary set about making some coffee. Starky flopped wearily into a chair. Suddenly his telephone rang. It sounded impatient and urgent. Wearily, Starky went into the hallway to answer the call. Mary wondered who would be calling so late. She watched the coffee percolator and thought how neat and methodical Starky had his kitchen arranged.

'Who are you?'

Starky's voice carried through the dividing unit which separated the kitchen from the hallway. Mary caught the irritation in his tone and turned in his direction. She saw him through an opening in the unit standing in the hallway and felt guilty at the thought that she was eavesdropping. She turned away.

'Help!... You can!... Who are you?'

Starky's voice sounded indignant. He was

getting heated.

'Tell me!'

Unable to stop herself, Mary's curiosity took over. She went to the doorway. She saw a strange, frozen look on Starky's face as if he was rigidly fixed to the voice at the other end. The bungalow could have collapsed around him, but his features would not have changed and the telephone would still have been in his hand, planted firmly against his ear.

'Katrina!' Starky gasped. Mary watched him. His eyes were wide open. 'Katrina?' Starky said again hoarsely, a look of incredulity taking over from the previous look of frozen anticipation.

'What the hell has she got to do with it?' Starky asked into the phone.

Mary heard a burble in the receiver. It sounded like a man's voice. Starky said, 'Why Russia?' in a hoarse voice. Mary didn't understand the gist of the conversation, but she had caught the feel of the electric tension in the atmosphere.

'Beasts,' Starky fumed into the red instrument. 'Guarantee?' he sneered.

Suddenly the conversation was over. There was a metallic click in the receiver. But Starky remained rooted to the spot as if

70

questioning whether the conversation he had just held, had ever taken place at all. Mary watched him slowly replace the receiver on its stand. Then, as if on impulse, he thumped the wall with his hand.

'Your coffee is in the kitchen,' Mary said gently. 'Is there anything the matter?'

Starky looked at her and through her. They went into the kitchen.

'There is your coffee.'

She handed him a cup. He sat down. He looked in a daze.

'Harry, you haven't spoken since you came off the phone,' Mary said, after a while.

Starky looked sullenly at his empty cup.

'What is it, Harry? Please tell me.'

Starky shook his head. She repeated her question.

'I don't know whether I can,' Starky said desperately and ran his hand through his hair.

'It has all got to do with that telephone call.'

Starky didn't answer. He lit a cigarette and smoked furiously.

'Well, if you won't talk to me about it,' Mary said sternly, 'tell the lieutenant.'

Starky looked up at her abruptly.

'What?' he asked.

'Tell the police,' Mary said again. 'If it is somebody threatening you, tell the police.'

'No!' Starky shouted. 'No!' He looked away from her. 'No, Mary,' he said quietly.

'Why not?' Mary asked. 'They will protect you.'

'Protect?' Starky asked. He came over and sat opposite her at the table. 'Mary, what did you overhear?'

'Not very much,' Mary smiled faintly. 'Who is Katrina?'

'Oh! no,' Starky groaned and started to pace the floor. Mary watched him patiently. The telephone started to ring again! Starky froze. He looked at Mary who smiled at him encouragingly. The phone continued to ring. He went over to the instrument in the hallway and picked up the receiver. Mary watched from the doorway.

'Hullo,' Starky said hoarsely.

Mary heard some message being relayed over the line. There was the metallic click again as the line abruptly went dead. Starky threw the receiver back on its stand and rushed into his bedroom. Mary followed him. Starky flung open his closet doors. There in front of them was a pale green silk dress! Laura Nolan's dress! Starky stood staring at it almost disbelieving what he saw.

72

So did Mary.

'Laura Nolan's!' she gasped.

Starky turned away and sat on the bed.

'That telephone call?' Mary asked.

Starky looked up at her.

'I didn't do it, Mary,' he said with feeling. 'Honestly, I didn't do it.'

'I believe you.'

'Someone is framing me.'

'Who is it, Harry?'

'I don't know,' he replied irritably.

'Then you must tell the police.'

Starky laughed scornfully.

'Police! How do you think they would react if they knew I had Laura Nolan's dress in my bungalow?' he scoffed. 'They would take the place apart and me with it. This would be the last nail in my coffin. And God knows what else they would find.'

He closed the closet doors.

'I need a drink,' he said.

Mary followed him into the lounge where he poured himself a stiff drink.

'Want one?'

Mary shook her head.

'Why should anyone want to frame you? Or threaten you?'

'I can't say,' he said, looking at her.

'Why not? I may be able to help.'

73

'Help? How?'

'Uncle George,' Mary said hesitantly. 'He has a lot of connections. He used to work for the F.B.I.'

Starky looked at her, genuinely surprised.

'Uncle George?'

'Yes. I told you about him.'

Starky shrugged, he didn't appear to recall her mentioning Uncle George.

'Couldn't he help?' Mary asked. 'Or get someone to help you?'

Starky sat silently staring into his glass as if tossing the thought around in his mind.

'Mary,' he said thoughtfully. 'Whoever was on that telephone would think that I was alone.'

'Yes, Harry.'

Starky stood up and looked around the room, saw that the drapes were drawn. That no one could see in.

'Your car is in the car port,' he said, 'where mine is normally parked.'

'Yes,' Mary agreed.

'It is a four door saloon like my own,' Starky went on. 'Not the same model, but not unlike. In the darkness no one would be able to tell the difference. So nobody would expect you to be here.'

'Don't you think you had better tell me

about it?' Mary asked. 'Otherwise I am an accessory.'

'Accessory?' Starky asked abruptly.

'Well, if I don't tell the police about the dress.'

Starky looked searchingly into her face.

'Please tell me, Harry.'

Starky sighed and shrugged.

'Mary,' he said slowly, as if searching for the correct words. 'When I was working in the U.K. I met a Polish girl. She belonged to the Polish community in London. She was the daughter of a refugee. We got married.'

A surprised look came over Mary's face, but she said nothing.

'We had a baby – a girl called Katrina,' Starky stammered. 'The marriage folded up. My wife left me for another Pole. She went back to Poland with this man, got a divorce and married him. That was seven years ago.'

'Have you heard from them since?' Mary asked, genuinely interested.

Starky shook his head.

'No, not a word.' He shrugged. 'There is no feeling between my ex-wife and myself. That finished when she left me, but my daughter... Well!' He threw his arms out in despair and let them flop by his side. 'That has hurt,' he said sadly. 'That has really hurt.' He gave a faint smile. 'That was one of the reasons why I went on the blinder last night. I was feeling a little sorry for myself.'

'I can understand now,' Mary said. 'Thanks for telling me.'

'That's just the beginning,' Starky said. 'The person on the telephone has me neatly framed for Laura Nolan's murder. He even has her clothes. Any time he likes he can drop an article – like her dress – right in my lap.'

'Why?' Mary asked seriously. 'Why?'

'Because somebody is working for the Communists!' Starky said forcibly.

'The Communists!' Mary gasped unbelievingly. 'The Communists!'

'Does it sound incredible?' Starky asked. 'Well, here is something more. If I don't do what I am told not only will I be framed for Laura Nolan's murder, but my daughter will be deported, with her mother, to a labour camp.'

'No!' Mary looked stunned. 'It can't be.'

'Can't it?' Starky asked. He gave a nervous laugh. 'It certainly can. They are like that.'

'If you help them what happens?' Mary asked. She had quickly got over the shock.

'I get the names of the cab driver and

another couple of witnesses to support my alibi, and my daughter remains in Warsaw where she is now living.'

'Blackmail!'

'Blackmail,' Starky agreed, 'and if I go to the police, there is no deal.'

'If the deal falls through, they wouldn't get what they wanted,' Mary said.

'Nobody wins,' Starky agreed, 'but I lose. They have the rest of Laura Nolan's clothes which they threaten to dump on me.'

'How would they know if you told the police?' Mary asked earnestly.

'I can't say,' Starky replied pensively. 'I wondered about that. Perhaps by what the police do, or they might even have an informer in the Police Force.' He looked sadly at her. 'Who knows? But would the lieutenant believe me?'

'Yes, he would, because I am your witness,' Mary said forcibly.

'Perhaps,' Starky said. 'Perhaps. But you only know what I have told you. You didn't overhear the whole of the conversation. If there was no follow up, the lieutenant would think we were just making it up.'

'Never mind,' Mary smiled encouragingly. 'We can work something out. I will ask Uncle George for help.'

Starky gave a faint smile.

'Sure,' he said. 'You can speak to Uncle George.' But by the tone of his voice he didn't seem to share Mary's faith in her uncle.

FIVE

Mary Lewis came out of the supermarket carrying the weekend groceries. It was the Saturday after Hendrich's party and Harry Starky's shattering telephone call.

'Here, let me help you,' a voice called out – a man's voice.

Mary stopped in her tracks and looked through her packages into the smiling, youthful face of a tall, slim man. He was raising his trilby politely. She saw fair hair, a happy face with laughing blue eyes and a warm smile.

'Oh!' Mary said, not sure of herself, or of the man.

'I'm here at Uncle George's request,' the man said lightly. Mary looked at the youthful figure in the neat, light grey suit and white shirt and said, 'Oh!' again.

The man took most of the parcels.

'But my father is collecting me,' Mary said, surprised at the way she was letting this man take charge.

'Was collecting you,' the man corrected

her. 'He has let me take his place.' They started to walk along the sidewalk.

'The car is over there,' the man said and indicated a light blue convertible. 'My name is Gary Maddison.'

She smiled faintly. 'How do you do? I am Mary Lewis.'

'Yes, I know.'

They walked towards the car.

'Are you a...?' Mary's question trailed away.

'Yes,' Maddison smiled and added gently, 'From Uncle George's old department.' Which wasn't quite true. Uncle George had been a records clerk whereas Maddison was an agent in Samuel Weiderman's department.

'I only asked Uncle George yesterday,' Mary said sheepishly.

'We act fast,' Maddison said lightly. Again that wasn't quite true. Maddison had been working on the Washington end of the case when the news of Laura Nolan's murder had reached Weiderman. Weiderman had immediately ordered Maddison to go to Medway Springs and he had been on his way when Uncle George had made his request. Weiderman had then contacted Maddison and changed tactics. Uncle George had provided them with a ready-made cover.

They reached the car. Maddison dumped the parcels on the rear seat and watched approvingly as Mary got into the passenger's seat. He liked what he saw – she looked so trim and pretty. Yes, he thought admiringly, it was his day.

He got in alongside her.

'Here are my credentials.' He showed her his identification card. She glanced at it apologetically. He seemed so young to be an F.B.I. agent, she thought. Not quite what she had expected.

'How is Uncle George?' Maddison asked.

'Oh! he is well, thank you,' Mary replied feeling more confident. 'He spends a lot of his time on the porch in the sun with his memories.'

Maddison smiled. He had a feeling that Uncle George had more than exaggerated his work for the Department, but he didn't say anything. He pulled away from the sidewalk and headed out of town.

'How did you know I was at the supermarket?' Mary asked.

'I called at your home. Your father told me. He also gave me your description.' Maddison looked at her and smiled. 'He told me to look for the prettiest girl in the town.'

Mary blushed up and turned her eyes away.

'Fathers are always like that,' she said.

'Well, yours was certainly telling the truth,' Maddison added.

They drove in silence.

'Is there anywhere we can talk over a drink? Maddison asked. 'I'm staying at Mrs Pringle's and I feel that she might have one ear on the keyhole.'

'She probably has,' Mary laughed. She felt strangely at ease with him, almost as if they were old friends, 'but she will certainly look after you. Why didn't you stay with us?'

'I didn't wish to burden you,' Maddison said lightly, skirting the real reason why he preferred to be independent, 'but I think it would arouse less suspicion if you introduced me around as your cousin from the East.' He flashed a smile at her. 'Tell them that I am passing through on my way to take up an appointment in San Francisco.'

'As what?' Mary asked seriously.

'A lawyer,' Maddison replied. 'I've just finished law school in New York and I'm having a holiday on my way West. O.K.?'

'Yes,' Mary agreed.

'Good. Now where can we talk?'

'Well, I had arranged to meet Harry at the

82

Country Club for lunch.'

'Harry Starky?'

'Yes.' Mary found herself blushing again and felt annoyed. 'He is going to take me flying at Jackson Field this afternoon. We could go to the Club and talk. I haven't arranged to meet him until mid-day.'

'Good,' Maddison agreed. 'I want to meet Mr Starky so we can kill two birds with one stone. We'll drop your parcels off first.'

'What do we tell Harry?' Mary asked hesitantly.

'The truth,' Maddison smiled.

'Oh!' Mary said and added, 'I'm so pleased.'

Maddison turned to look at her.

'Are you stuck on the guy?' he asked.

'No,' Mary said flushing up. 'We are just...'

'Good friends?' Maddison asked.

'Yes,' Mary said firmly. He had no right to question her like that, she thought. It was none of his business how she felt about Harry. None at all. She pouted her mouth and sat back in her seat. How did she feel towards Harry? she asked herself. They were good friends. She would even have gone further. She liked him very much indeed, but was she stuck on him as Maddison had suggested? She didn't know. Or did she? she asked herself. Was she evading the issue?

The remainder of the drive to Mary's home and the Country Club was more formal, during which Maddison asked a number of questions on direction and Mary answered. However, when they arrived at the Club, Maddison took charge in a friendly, patronising manner.

'Remember, I am your cousin from the East,' he said quietly, but firmly. 'You are pleased to be with me. Smile at people and introduce me to whoever you wish.'

He took hold of her arm and led her across the gravel drive to the terrace where a number of people sat watching the more energetic club members in the swimming pool.

They sat at a table.

'Tell me what it is all about,' he said casually. 'In your own words.'

'Well, it is really about Harry,' Mary said.

'Just start at the beginning,' Maddison said patiently.

Slowly, carefully picking her words, Mary explained how she had returned to Harry Starky's bungalow and overheard some of the telephone conversation, and of what he had told her.

Maddison questioned her about details

until he had a full, clear picture.

'And Starky hasn't informed the police?' he asked.

'No,' Mary shook her head. 'They said they would know immediately if he spoke to them and his daughter would suffer. The deal would be off.'

'But he knows you were going to contact Uncle George?'

'Yes,' Mary said.

'What do you think he would have done if you hadn't been there?'

'Harry is a very worried man,' Mary said with feeling. 'He is sure the police suspect him of Laura Nolan's murder and now he knows that someone is prepared to frame him and harm his daughter.'

'You haven't answered my question,' Maddison persisted.

'I don't know,' Mary said honestly.

'Would he have contacted us?' Maddison asked. 'It is important.'

'I don't think so,' Mary said hesitantly. 'I don't know what he would have done. He doesn't want any harm to come to his daughter.'

'Which is understandable,' Maddison said. 'Has he had any further messages from them?'

'I think so, but I'm not certain. I phoned him last night and he was pretty evasive. It made me think that they had been at him again.'

'Did you ask?'

'Yes, but he didn't confirm or deny it.'

Maddison relaxed in his seat and felt the warm sun on his face. It was an incredible piece of good fortune that they had got wind of Starky's blackmail through Mary. So good in fact that he wondered whether the slip had been intentional. After his talk with Mary he was still uncertain. If Starky had been alone when the call had been made Starky would probably be working for the opposition. But Starky hadn't been alone and he was now working for the F.B.I. Was that just a lucky break? Maddison didn't know.

'If anyone had been watching the bungalow,' he said, 'when you returned from the party with Starky, would they have seen you?'

'No,' Mary replied without hesitation. 'It was a dark night. We parked in the drive in the car port which screens the road. The drapes were drawn in the kitchen so no one could see me.'

'Unless they knew Starky had no car,' Maddison said.

86

'His car had been returned by the garage mechanics earlier that afternoon. It was in his garage.'

So if there had been anyone from the estate keeping an eye on Starky's where-abouts, Maddison thought, they would know his car had been returned. When he later returned from the party they would think he was alone.

'What happened when you left to return to your own home?' Maddison asked.

'It was much later,' Mary replied. 'There was no one about. No one would know who it was.'

It was unlikely that whoever had made the call would be keeping a twenty-four hour watch on Starky, Maddison thought. So they were in the position of knowing that Starky was being set up by Communist agents without them being aware that they knew. Or was that what somebody wanted them to believe? He wondered how Starky would behave. It was no good Starky kid-ding himself that he could save his kid. Whatever the promises they had made to Starky there was going to be no means of seeing that they kept to their word. As far as Maddison and the F.B.I. were concerned, Starky was essential to the internal security of the country and had to be used to that end.

When Starky arrived at the Club, Maddison could understand why Mary could be attracted to him, and also how the happenings of the past forty-eight hours were affecting him. His features were homely, honest looking and troubled. His shoulders sagged and his brow was constantly furrowed. He chain smoked and had an air of nervous tension about him, as if the electric chair was just around the corner. Maddison immediately felt sympathetic towards the man.

Mary made the introductions. Starky sat at their table and ordered a round of drinks.

'Mary filled you in?' he asked.

'Some,' Maddison replied. 'Not all.'

Starky frowned.

'If anything happens to my daughter,' he said sadly, 'I will never forgive myself.'

'You realise, of course, that even if you did as they ask, there is no guarantee that they will leave your daughter alone.'

Starky smoked his cigarette, nervously.

'My ex-wife was on the phone last night,' he said.

'On the telephone?' Mary asked.

'Yes. Not in person. It was a tape recording.'

They were really putting the pressure on, Maddison thought.

'She said that they had promised to restore their full rights and let them leave the country if I help them. They want to come to the States. Otherwise they will be sent to a labour camp.'

'And do you think they will keep their word?' Maddison asked.

Starky sighed and shook his head.

'I've given this a hell of a lot of thought,' he said sadly. 'It never left me all night.' He pressed his cigarette into the ash tray and lit a fresh one.

'And?' Maddison asked.

'I've come to the conclusion that I'm a loser either way. Theirs or yours.'

'How come?'

'Well, if I help them there is no guarantee that they will keep their word, and if I do something contrary to the laws of this country I am a wanted man and a sucker for further blackmail.'

'But if you help us you are saving yourself,' Maddison said quietly.

'Yes,' Starky agreed. 'I have no alternative now. Have I?'

'No,' Maddison agreed, 'you haven't. For what it is worth, I think the Communists are using your daughter and your ex-wife for their own ends. There is no guarantee, as you say, that they will do what they promise and there is no guarantee, in fact, that your daughter, or your ex-wife, is in any danger.'

'Yeah,' Starky agreed. 'I figured it that way also.' He again smiled at Mary. 'In fact,' he added, 'if Mary had not been with me in the bungalow at the time of the first call no one would even believe that I had been contacted. It would just have been between me and them.'

Maddison didn't ask which way Starky would have gone in that situation, but he had his own thoughts on the subject. Instead he said, 'That is our trump card and we must capitalise on it. No one knows who I am, or why I am here. We must keep it that way.'

'Yeah!' Starky finished off his drink.

'What happened on the night of Laura Nolan's murder?' Maddison asked.

Starky told him as he had told the lieutenant. Maddison listened in silence until he had finished.

'Think carefully,' Maddison said. 'Who could possibly have known in advance that you were going to have a blinder?'

'A lot of people,' Mary answered for

Starky. 'He refused an invitation to one of our staff's twenty-first celebration a week ago because he said that he was going out to celebrate his fortieth birthday.'

'Yeah, that's true,' Starky agreed.

'Did you mention where you were going to celebrate it?' Maddison asked.

Starky shook his head.

'Have you used Luigi's saloon before?'

'Sure!'

'On your own?'

'No. I called in once with Jayson Hendrich on our way back from Jackson Field, and once with Dr Kay.'

'Dr Kay?' Maddison asked.

'We were going to the football game,' Starky explained. 'We were early.'

'He's British, isn't he?' Maddison asked.

'Yeah,' Starky agreed. 'Said he had never been to a football game so I offered to take him.'

'Hm,' Maddison said thoughtfully. 'So they could have talked.'

'I'm afraid so,' Starky agreed. 'I went back to Luigi's last night,' he sighed, 'hoping to pick up something that might help. I even had a word with Ma Hollings.'

'Ma Hollings?' Maddison asked.

'She runs a friendly house in the sticks,'

Starky said and looked apologetically at Mary. 'If you know what I mean. One of her girls was in the bar when I was there on the night of Laura Nolan's murder.'

'Get anywhere?' Maddison asked.

Starky shook his head.

'Ma Hollings keeps a tight lip,' he said regretfully. 'I did learn that it was Fin Neilson's silver wedding anniversary the night he was off duty. He's the regular bartender. The guy that stood in for him was some guy from Chicago who had been up here on vacation.'

'Did you get his description?' Maddison asked.

'Yeah,' Starky frowned. 'And it doesn't tie up with what I can remember of the guy.' He threw up his arms in despair.

'Have you any idea at all who might be behind all this?' Maddison asked earnestly.

Starky shook his head sadly.

'No,' he said.

'Did you recognise anything about the voice on the phone?'

Again Starky shook his head. 'No,' he sighed. 'It was a man's voice, but not one I can place.'

There was a short pause and then Maddison asked, 'But you know what they are after?'

'Yeah!' Starky said grimly. 'They want information abut the research at the plant.'

'Can you give it to them?' Maddison asked.

'No,' Starky said, inhaling his cigarette. 'The security at the centre is cast iron. I have no means of getting at any classified information.'

'You are allowed in the lab area?'

'Yeah, but always escorted.'

Maddison looked thoughtful.

'There are two possible thoughts on this,' he said quietly. Mary and Starky looked at him deeply interested. 'Either the person who is setting you up is unfamiliar with the security set up at the plant and thinks that you can get hold of the information they need.'

'Or?' Mary asked.

'Someone at the plant who knows what the information is, wants a scapegoat to pass it on to.'

'Why should they do that?' Mary asked.

'Yeah,' Starky agreed. 'If it is someone at the plant why don't they just give it to their contact?'

'How many people would have access to such information?' Maddison asked. 'Or could get at it?'

'Oh! Five or six at the most,' Starky replied. 'The Director, the four scientists and possibly McIntyre.'

'Six prominent people,' Maddison said forcefully. 'If one of them is a Communist sympathiser, or more likely a Communist agent, then I am sure that the Communists are going to see that he is fully protected. The information they want must be very vital to them otherwise they wouldn't go to the extent they have to set you up. But if one of those six is in their camp, then their future is too bright to foul it up.'

Mary and Starky exchanged glances. There was a puzzled and worried expression on both their faces.

'It may, of course, be the first possibility,' Starky said quietly.

'I doubt it,' Maddison replied.

'Why?' Mary asked.

'The timing,' Maddison explained. 'When did the final tests take place?'

'A few days ago,' Starky said.

'And the final report?'

'Is to be finished by the end of next week,' Starky added.

'Seven days,' Maddison said lightly. 'After that the project is finished. It is out of the unit's hands.'

'Yes,' Starky sighed. 'Seven days.' He

looked as if they were going to be the long-
est seven days in his life.

'Don't worry,' Mary said. 'It will come all
right in the end.'

'Sure,' Starky agreed, and gave a faint
smile. 'I only wish Lieutenant Hugan believed in me.'

'He will,' Maddison said encouragingly.
'In time.'

SIX

Maddison sat in his convertible and looked along the tree lined avenue. It was like a film setting. The roadway was verged with grass and trees and the detached dwellings were surrounded by neat lawns and shrubbery. There were the usual noises – lawns being cut, dogs barking and children shouting. A typical fringe of town estate.

Satisfied that he was not being watched, Maddison got out of his car and walked along the sidewalk and up the path to one of the buildings. Before he reached the entrance door, he saw the fly screen open and a slim man of medium build appear on the veranda. He had a scraggy, tough face and grey hair to match. He was in his shirt sleeves and held a can of beer in his hand. He looked as if the heat bothered him.

Maddison mounted the steps. The man watched him.

'Lieutenant Hugan?' Maddison asked.

'Yeah,' the man frowned. Maddison could feel an immediate antagonism towards himself from the lieutenant, and wondered whether it was because of his invasion of the policeman's privacy.

'My name is Maddison.' He felt in his pocket for his credentials.

The lieutenant eyed him up and down almost contemptuously. 'F.B.I.?' he asked, before Maddison had shown him his identification.

Maddison nodded his head in agreement. For a moment the two men just stood looking at each other. The elderly policeman and the youthful Federal man.

'Your first assignment?' Hugan asked.

Maddison blushed up.

'On my own,' he admitted. 'I have been on others.'

'I suppose you had better come in,' the lieutenant sighed. He walked into his house leaving Maddison to follow. Maddison wondered what had fouled up the lieutenant's day.

Inside the house, Maddison had a strange feeling that something was wrong. The furniture and decorations looked as if they belonged to a comfortable family, where grandchildren would be welcome, but there was an uneasy feeling of sadness about. As he turned to follow the lieutenant into a side room, a woman appeared. Maddison took her to be the lieutenant's wife. She was slim, petite, with grey hair like her husband. Her face looked sad and drawn, her eyes red rimmed. She was wearing a silk dress which looked as if it had been quickly thrown on.

Maddison smiled at her.

'Good afternoon,' he said warmly. 'I am Gary Maddison.'

The lieutenant scowled from across the room.

'Mrs Hugan,' he explained.

'I am very sorry to invade upon your privacy on such a nice afternoon, Mrs Hugan,' Maddison said apologetically, and gave her a disarming smile.

The woman warmed to his youthful appeal.

'That's all right, Mr Maddison, my husband was going to business.' She returned Maddison's smile.

'We can talk in here,' the lieutenant said gruffly.

'Would you like a can of beer?' Mrs Hugan asked.

Maddison turned to her. 'That would be real nice,' he said with feeling.

'I'll get it,' Hugan scowled and wondered what had made his wife make the suggestion. It wasn't like her.

'Are you here on business, Mr Maddison?' Mrs Hugan asked.

'Yes,' Maddison smiled, 'but I hope I won't have to bother you.'

'This is no bother,' Mrs Hugan said. 'We have few visitors these days.'

The lieutenant returned with a can of beer and a glass, and took Maddison into his study and closed the door. Again Maddison got the impression of a room which had seen better days and happier times. On top of a wall fitting stood a photograph of a young man in the uniform of an Army officer. The lieutenant's son? Maddison wondered.

'Why the social call?' Hugan asked gruffly. 'Did you call at Headquarters?'

'No,' Maddison replied. 'I don't want anyone to know that I am here.'

Hugan showed his displeasure.

'Mind telling me why?'

'Not at the moment,' Maddison replied. 'Give it a couple of days.'

'Where are you staying?'

'At Mrs Pringle's, on the South Ridge Estate. I'm on a vacation from the East.'

The lieutenant finished off his beer.

'My sergeant is picking me up in half an hour,' he said pointedly. 'What's on your mind.'

'Harry Starky,' Maddison replied.

The lieutenant stretched his mouth, baring his teeth. It was a habit he had developed when he wished to show displeasure.

'I could nail a rap on him this afternoon,' he growled, 'and make it stick.'

'Homicide?'

'First degree.'

Maddison slowly drank his beer to let the lieutenant's emotions settle down.

'On what grounds?' he asked.

The lieutenant gave Maddison a look which suggested that he hadn't time to teach a fresh F.B.I. man his job.

'His alibi has no foundation,' he said gruffly. 'It doesn't tie up. No substantiation. No one can confirm that he was in the bar. There is no cab driver to confirm that he took him home in his drunken state.'

'And no one to deny it?' Maddison said.

'No,' Hugan growled. He flipped a cigarette out of his packet and lit it. 'I have a hunch about Starky,' he added.

'Well, Lieutenant,' Maddison said evenly, 'I don't get hunches. I haven't been in the game long enough. I work on facts.'

'O.K.,' Hugan said aggressively. 'Suppose you give me some of your facts. Tell me why that crew at the plant needs a full time nursemaid? Tell me about McIntyre's reports to Washington. Give me some facts.'

'Sorry, Lieutenant,' Maddison said apologetically. 'My hands are tied right now.'

Hugan showed his displeasure.

'What's your next move?' he growled.

'That depends upon a number of things,' Maddison replied evasively. He stood up. 'I shall be back to see you,' he added.

'Here or at the station? I prefer to keep my work away from my home.'

The lieutenant gave Maddison a stern look to reinforce his point.

'I can appreciate that,' Maddison agreed. 'Unfortunately it may not be possible. I do not wish to broadcast my presence here for a number of reasons.'

The lieutenant scowled.

'However,' Maddison added, 'I shall try to make my visits as brief as possible.'

The lieutenant also stood up. He was much smaller than Maddison, but his height had never been a drawback to the lieutenant.

'You will tell Mrs Hugan not to mention my visit,' Maddison said hesitantly.

'She never talks about my business,' Hugan replied gruffly. He opened the door pointedly. Maddison hesitated before leaving.

'Just one thing, Lieutenant,' he said.

'Yeah?'

'I don't think Starky is your man.'

The lieutenant looked Maddison straight in the eyes.

'Don't you be fooled by what I said about my hunches,' he growled. 'I know my job. One thing I have learned, Maddison, is that if you check back far enough you will find the motive, and when you've got that you are half way there. Another thing I have learned is to have a flexible mind.' He continued to stare Maddison in the eyes. 'I've had nearly forty years with the Force,' he added. 'I know my job.'

'It was just a thought,' Maddison said apologetically.

'You a College kid?'

'I was at College,' Maddison replied.

'What did they teach you there?' Hugan asked.

Maddison looked at the lieutenant unflinchingly.

'To think, Lieutenant,' he said. 'To think.'

Before the lieutenant could further the point, Maddison had left the room. The lieutenant raised his eyebrows begrudgingly and gave the faintest flicker of a smile. The kid had a point, he thought. He looked out of the window and saw Maddison on the pathway talking to Madge. He watched them talking. Maddison was explaining something about the plants. Madge was listening intently. He turned his back on them and gritted his teeth. He had suddenly got a picture of Danny standing there. Had Madge also got the same impression? he wondered. For a moment he stood deep in thought and then clenched his fists and thumped the back of the chair as if trying to erase some memory from his mind.

SEVEN

Helen Logan slowly brushed her hair and stared thoughtfully in the mirror. Saturday night at the Country Club had become a routine introduced by her husband to bring the unit closer together on a social basis. She didn't question the sincerity of her husband's intentions, but she questioned the value of continuing the gathering. It had developed into a pattern of behaviour which Helen Logan was finding boring.

They would gather in the bar and the men would ply themselves with drinks. When Helen Logan felt she could stand it no longer, she would catch her husband's eye and the party would have dinner. By this time the effect of the drinks would have loosened the tongues and the conversation would be more worldly, especially when Jayson Hendrich was with them.

Unconsciously Helen Logan brushed her hair with more vigour as she thought about Jayson Hendrich. She found him uncouth and repulsive. Yet in a strange way he excited her. She could never imagine herself in bed with him, but at the same time the very thought of such an act stirred some of her feelings. Now Peter Kay and Harry Starky were different, she thought. They were more her type, especially Kay. He was sophisticated, easy to talk to and clean cut. She would have liked to have an affair with one of them. She might even do that yet, she mused. With Peter Kay, she thought. He had no ties. Starky had always had Mary Lewis around him.

Through her mirror she caught sight of her husband dressing. There was something worrying him, she thought. She recognised the signs. It would be that bitch, Laura Nolan. Had there been anything between her husband and Laura Nolan? she wondered. There had been those two occasions when Laura Nolan had been visiting Chicago the same time as her husband. The coincidence had been suspicious, but that was all Helen Logan had to go on. Her husband often had to visit Washington and Chicago.

The movement of the brush through her hair became slower. There had also been those telephone calls recently. What had they been about? she wondered. Who had it been? Why had he been so evasive? And the night of Laura Nolan's murder. Had he been at home all night as he said? She brushed her hair more vigorously. Whatever else she might think about her husband, he was no murderer. She sighed. If only she could be free of him. He was too stiff, too dull. She longed for fun, enjoyment. She still felt young enough to do things, to be attractive to people, to be liked. Her husband kept her confined along his narrow path of respectability. Their life at Medway Springs had become a dreary routine, but she played along with it because she wanted to get back to Washington. She wanted the project at the plant to be a success. She wanted her husband to reap the rewards. She wanted nothing to stand in his way. That was why she played her role with apparent conviction. And there was the Senator. He was in Washington waiting for her. Now, he was her type of man. And he would go far. Maybe even to the top.

Whilst Helen Logan was enjoying her mental gymnastics, Joe McIntyre was standing on the lawn of his bungalow smoking the third cigarette in a chain that had only started a few minutes earlier when he had arrived with their baby sitter.

McIntyre had things on his mind. He always had these days, but now he had the Laura Nolan business in addition. He happened to catch sight of his wife through the kitchen window. She was preparing the sitter's supper. Momentarily his thoughts were side tracked. His wife liked her Saturday night at the Club, he thought. She also liked Medway Springs. But come to think of it, she liked most things and most people. She even liked Senator Leebright. McIntyre flipped his cigarette to the ground, stood on it, and lit another one. Yes, she even liked the Senator, he thought. So did the kids – Uncle Douglas to them. McIntyre scowled. The Senator was like a monkey forever on his back. There was even that photograph of the Senator and McIntyre together, in uniform, on top of the bureau. If only he could throw off the Senator, he thought. If only he had enough dough to be free of him. If only one of his long shots would come off… He shook his head sadly. Those thoughts were nothing new to him. He had lived with them a long time now. He turned his mind back to the two other problems which had been occupying his attention. Number one was Laura Nolan, and number two was the F.B.I.

Laura Nolan had troubled him for some

time. He had said so in his reports. She had been a funny kid, all mixed up. There had been something bothering her. He had nearly got it out of her on the night before she was murdered. If only Benson and Starky hadn't come on the scene. What the hell had she been going to tell him? It was all tied up with the work at the Centre – and her murder. Her murder! Surely the F.B.I. must have been informed. Why the hell hadn't they put in an appearance? They must know about the project and how important it was that any information didn't get into the wrong hands. What the hell were they playing at? Or was the Senator playing it cool? McIntyre knew how ambitious the Senator was; how far he wanted to go; how far he was prepared to go to get it. The Laura Nolan business could upset his plans. So could the project if it got fouled up. The Senator would bounce back again like a rubber ball, but it would delay things. Perhaps he had persuaded the F.B.I. to play it cool until it was all over and then allow the Senator to move in and stir it up? Or was the F.B.I. not wanting to rock the boat? Another week and McIntyre's responsibilities would be finished. Another week!

'Joe!' his wife called to him from the

kitchen window. 'You had better come and get changed,' she said. 'And see what Lee wants, honey.'

'O.K.' McIntyre said.

He threw away the cigarette. He would give the F.B.I. a further twenty-four hours, he thought. If they didn't put in an appearance, he would contact them direct. Security was his responsibility. They might be waiting for him to make the move. Trying him out.

They were all at the Club when Maddison arrived with Mary and Starky. Starky had been contacted again. Another threat to his ex-wife and daughter. He was in a sombre mood. But not so the rest of the party. It was as if they had been looking for an escape from the cloud hanging over them and had found it at the bar. They were sinking their drinks fast. Mary introduced Maddison as her cousin from the East and they accepted him without question. Maddison quickly appraised the gathering. He immediately recognised Logan's commanding officer role and his wife's desire to be liked and admired. Jayson Hendrich was boisterous and arrogant, whilst his wife was quiet and demure. McIntyre sat back and said little. He appeared content so long as his glass was full and his wife was talking. The Ludvicks were less jovial than the rest of the party. Dr Ludvick kept close to Logan and Frieda Ludvick, who was a shapely, attractive woman in her late forties, talked to Janet McIntyre in her clipped foreign accent. Kay looked as if he had started drinking early and was all set to have a ball.

Maddison watched and took part. He saw Mary's concern for Starky as Starky tried to drown his troubles with alcohol. Peter Kay and Helen Logan became physically closer to each other. Hendrich talked to everyone, mainly about himself, and McIntyre just drank.

It would have just been another evening at the Club if it hadn't been for Laura Nolan's murder. They never talked about it, but it was nevertheless there waiting to catch up with their hangovers.

For Starky the evening took on an unexpected twist when a waiter came to the table and told him he was wanted on the telephone. It was at a time when there was only McIntyre, Starky, Mary and Maddison at the table.

'Excuse me,' Starky mumbled. He pushed his chair back and left the table.

'Say, why don't you two have a dance?'

McIntyre said benevolently to Maddison and Mary. 'That'll give me an opportunity to get a quick drink.'

Mary turned to Maddison.

'Shall we?' Maddison asked.

'Love to,' Mary smiled.

They walked over to the small dance floor. Maddison took hold of Mary.

'Where are the telephones?' he asked.

'In the foyer next to the cocktail bar,' Mary explained. She looked at him. 'Do you think that...'

'No,' Maddison said, 'but just in case, do you mind if we cut the dance?'

'Of course not,' Mary said.

They left the floor and walked into the foyer as Starky was closing the door of the telephone booth.

Starky had gone to the telephone very uncertain as to who would be on the other end. Hesitantly, he picked up the receiver.

'Your call, Mr Starky,' the Club operator said, and switched the call through.

Starky breathed heavily. 'Starky,' he said.

'Good evening, Mr Starky,' a voice said – an Irish voice!

'Do you know who is speaking?' the voice drawled.

'No,' Starky lied.

'I am the man who drove you to your bungalow from Luigi's saloon the other night.'

'Who are you?' Starky asked cautiously, his brain working overtime.

The voice gave a chuckle.

'Listen, mister,' it said, 'there is something funny going on and I want out.'

'Who are you?' Starky asked again. 'Where can I meet you?'

'Take it easy,' the voice drawled. 'All in good time.'

Starky grimly held the phone. He caught sight of Maddison and Mary in the foyer.

'As I was saying, Mr Starky, there is something going on which I don't understand.'

'What?' Starky asked. 'Tell me what.'

The voice chuckled down the line.

'How much are you prepared to pay?'

Starky scowled. Blackmail! He caught Maddison's eye and motioned his head, indicating that Maddison should join him.

'That depends on what you have to sell,' he said. With his foot he opened the booth door. Maddison stood outside with his back to the booth and lit a cigarette.

'I want three hundred bucks by tomorrow evening,' the voice said. 'In singles. Can you get it?'

'Perhaps.'

113

'Listen, mister. I'm doing you a favour. Get hold of that money and I'll talk to you, but only to you. Mister, you are in some jam.'

'Where do I see you?' Starky asked.

'I'll tell you that tomorrow. I'll phone you early in the morning. Get the dough.'

'How did you know where to contact me?' Starky asked hurriedly.

'I know more about you than you know yourself,' came the reply. 'Just get the dough.'

The phone went abruptly dead. Maddison rejoined Mary as Logan and Kay strolled into the foyer. Kay appeared interested in their whereabouts.

'This is where you had got to,' he said lightly. Maddison wondered why he had been concerned. 'We're just going for a breath of fresh air.'

Logan smiled at them and the two scientists left the foyer. When Starky came over to them Maddison forestalled any remark.

'Let's go and have a drink,' he said and ushered Mary and Starky into the bar.

Starky explained about the call.

'That was the cab driver I was telling you about,' he said excitedly hardly able to contain himself. He looked at Maddison. 'You heard him?'

'Yeah,' Maddison agreed. 'I heard him.'

'Thank goodness for that,' Starky said. 'At least it proves that he was not a figment of my imagination.'

'We believed you, Harry,' Mary said quietly.

'Yeah,' Starky agreed apologetically. 'He has something to sell,' he added. 'Wants three hundred bucks.' He took a long drink. 'It'll be worth it to get my hands on him. Now perhaps the lieutenant will believe me.'

'Do you think he will be prepared to make a statement?' Maddison asked quietly.

Starky held his glass to his mouth and looked at Maddison thoughtfully.

'No,' he sighed. 'He probably won't.'

'What are the arrangements?' Maddison asked.

'He is going to contact me again early in the morning, to give me the details. I have to get three hundred dollars together in singles.'

'Can you?'

'Yeah. I can get hold of some from the plant.' Again he took a long drink. 'What do we do?' he asked.

'Wait for the call,' Maddison said.

'What about the lieutenant?' Starky asked. 'Shouldn't we bring him in on this? At least he can overhear the call.'

It was Maddison's turn to play with his glass.

'No,' he said firmly. 'Remember your contact warned against talking to the cops. They might be putting up a bluff, but on the other hand, they might just have a link. Leave the cops out of it. We don't want to foul it up. You have a witness to the call.'

'You?' Starky asked.

'Me,' Maddison agreed.

'Well, take care,' Starky warned. 'You and Mary are precious to me.'

'Don't worry,' Maddison smiled. 'Now you and Mary go and join the party or they'll become suspicious.'

'O.K. Come on, Mary.'

Starky led Mary back to the dining room. Maddison watched them go and then went to the reception counter. The switch board girl was a young, brassy blonde chewing gum. She didn't quite fit in with the Club's image. She eyed Maddison curiously, looking him up and down. Maddison withdrew a five dollar note and placed it on the counter in front of her.

'There has just been a call for Mr Starky,' he said. She eyed him coolly. 'Any idea where it was from?' He released the five dollar note. It disappeared in beside the girl's bosom.

'It was an out of town call,' she drawled.

'Long distance?' Maddison asked.

The girl shook her head. 'Out of town, Little Hampton or Railton. Something like that.'

'How do you figure that?'

'The operator's accent was local.'

Bright kid, Maddison thought.

'Tell me anything else about it?'

She chewed a while.

'There was the sound of traffic. Came from a filling station or the like.'

'Did he ask for Mr Starky by name?'

'Yeah.'

'He knew he was here?'

'Seemed to.'

'Did you get his accent?'

'Sure, it was easy. He was Irish.'

'Thanks,' Maddison smiled, and turned to walk away.

'Say what gives?' the girl asked.

Maddison swung round. 'What do you mean?' he asked.

'Why all the interest? You're the second.'

'Second?'

'Yeah. I've made more in the last ten minutes than I make in tips all week.'

Maddison flung another five dollar note across the counter.

'Here is some more,' he said. 'Who else was asking?'

117

Again the note disappeared into her bosom.

'Mr McIntyre,' she drawled, 'but he wasn't so direct as you.' She gave him an inviting look. 'Or as interesting.'

McIntyre! Why should he be interested? Maddison wondered. Was he just doing his job as Security Officer? Or was there another reason?

'Thanks,' he said.

Maddison walked slowly back to the dining room. The band was in full swing and the dance floor vibrated to the beat. Logan and Kay had rejoined the party. Logan was in deep conversation with Ludvick and Hendrich. McIntyre was dancing with his wife. Kay and Helen Logan appeared to be very happy to be in such close proximity with each other on the dance floor. Starky was throwing Mary about as if a weight had been lifted from his shoulders. Emily Hendrich was talking to Freda Ludvick. It all appeared innocent. Was it one of them who was pushing Starky? Maddison wondered. Was one of them actually in the pay of the Russians? It didn't seem conceivable, but he had been in the Department long enough to know that anything was possible in the espionage business.

EIGHT

Harry Starky's Sunday was not as he would have planned it, or as he had hoped. From the very beginning he had a feeling that all was not going to go well. It was a hot, sultry day. The type of day when the perspiration and the liquid intake keep up a continuous battle to dissipate the energy of the human body. And Harry Starky hadn't slept well. In fact he hadn't had a really good night's sleep since Laura Nolan's murder. He had developed a pain at the nape of his neck which periodically wouldn't give up. That Sunday morning was one of its big days.

After an early coffee breakfast he sat, smoked, and waited. The only relief to his vigil was to watch the antics of Diana Bradley whom he could see through his kitchen window. She flitted into his vision in various stages of undress as she performed her domestic chores. It kept him amused, but after a while he began to wonder if she wasn't doing it on purpose. Perhaps, he thought, the heat was affecting her.

By ten o'clock the pain at the back of his neck had eased, but there had been no call from his cabbie. Starky had promised to phone Maddison immediately he had been contacted. Shortly before eleven Maddison phoned him. When the phone rang Starky's pulse didn't increase a beat.

'Anything happen yet?' Maddison asked.

'No,' Starky growled. 'He said he would contact me first thing this morning. So far – no joy.'

'There could be difficulties at the other end,' Maddison warned. 'You had better stay with it. Call Mary as soon as anything breaks.'

'Sure.'

Starky replaced the phone. He could feel the frustration swelling inside of him. He sat on the terrace with a bottle of rye and stared hard at Diana Bradley whose tight fitting jeans and tee shirt accentuated the full curves of her figure. She was aware that Starky was watching her. She even had a good idea what was in his mind, and it pleased her.

After Maddison had spoken to Starky on the telephone, he motored slowly through the town and into the district where Lieutenant Hugan lived. It hadn't surprised him that Starky had not been contacted. It was something he had suspected would happen. He parked the car in the shade of an overhanging tree and watched the trickle of residents make their way to the church, all dressed in their finery. When the church service had got under way, he walked up to Hugan's house and rang the door bell. Hugan appeared, unshaven, in an old pair of slacks and tee shirt. He opened the door.

'Come on in,' he said, neither friendly nor unfriendly. 'I've been expecting you.'

'Thought perhaps you might have gone to church,' Maddison remarked as he entered the house.

'Mrs Hugan does the praying in this house.' Hugan ushered Maddison into the kitchen. 'Coffee?'

'Yeah.'

Maddison put his trilby on the bench and sat on a stool. Hugan wasn't so aggressive as he had been at their last meeting. He handed Maddison the coffee.

'Settled the case yet?' Hugan asked.

Maddison shook his head. 'No, have you?'

'I have my theories,' Hugan growled, 'but they are not conclusive – yet!'

'Pretty certain?' Maddison asked.

Hugan raised his eyebrows and shrugged.

'Enjoy yourself last night?' he asked. 'At the Country Club?'

'Keeping tabs on me?' Maddison asked.

'Not you,' Hugan said without any let up of his rugged expression. 'Them.'

'They seemed to enjoy themselves,' Maddison said.

'So I gather. Surprising how little effect the murder has had on them. I wonder which one is putting on the big act?'

'What makes you so sure it's one of them?'

'Oh, it's one of them all right.'

Hugan drank his coffee.

'What have you come to tell me today, Mr F.B.I. man?' he asked.

'I'm not trying to teach you your job,' Maddison said politely.

'Say, that's good of you.'

'I just want to put you in the picture so we can get them together.'

'Them?' Hugan asked.

'Them,' Maddison agreed.

'O.K. Suppose you fill me in.'

'Starky is on the receiving end of a plot to get access to some very secret information,' Maddison said slowly.

'Say, what do you know!' Hugan raised his eyebrows mockingly. 'Right here in Medway Springs. Well, I never!'

Maddison flushed up.

'It's true, damn you!'

'O.K., O.K.' Hugan changed his attitude. 'I don't doubt the truth of your remark, but you must admit it comes as a shock.'

'Yes,' Maddison said. 'I agree.'

Hugan poured out some fresh coffee.

'O.K. kid, let's have it. Fill me in. From the beginning. Why a small place like Medway Springs for instance?'

Maddison drank the coffee.

'When Dr Cusack was at Columbia University,' he said quietly, 'he published a paper suggesting a line of research which could produce a cheaper type of fuel suitable for rocket projectory. The Defence Department were interested, but they thought it was a long shot. The Research Centre at the Amalgamated Chemical Plant here at Medway Springs was available and within the budget allocated to the project. So Cusack was given a team of scientists and set to work under Dr Logan and the watchful eye of the Senate Committee. The project was given top security, no publicity, and poor odds on success.'

'But Cusack came up with something?' Hugan suggested.

Maddison nodded his head. 'There were

some tests made last month in Florida. The findings are being kept secret, but they must be hopeful.'

'Go on,' Hugan said.

'A short while ago a Russian agent in Berlin came over to our side,' Maddison explained seriously. 'The C.I.A. got a lot of useful information out of him. One piece was passed to my Department. It was that the K.G.B., the Russian spy network, knows a hell of a lot of what is going on at the Research Centre here in Medway Springs. They have been given orders to get a copy of the report on the results of the research.'

Hugan looked impressed.

'And Starky is being got at to get hold of the secrets?' Hugan asked with less cynicism than before.

'Yes,' Maddison said.

'Why didn't you tell me this yesterday? Why has Starky not told us?' Hugan asked sharply, a deep frown across his brow.

'It is by pure chance that I came into it,' Maddison explained. 'Starky was contacted by telephone last Thursday. The day after Laura Nolan's murder. Mary Lewis just happened to be in the bungalow at the time. It was after a party at Jayson Hendrich's place.'

'Happened?' Hugan asked. There was a strong air of doubt in the lieutenant's tone.

'Her car is like Starky's. She drove him home after the party and went in for a coffee. It was late. Whoever phoned might have expected Starky to be alone.'

'Go on.' Hugan was deeply interested.

'Her uncle used to be a clerk in one of our departments.'

'So she told him and he contacted the Bureau,' Hugan said.

'Yes.'

'Why did they pick Starky?'

'Don't you know?' Maddison smiled.

'Maybe. We back checked. He has an ex-wife and nine year old kid now living in Poland.'

'They've threatened to make them suffer if Starky doesn't co-operate.'

'They play rough.'

'Very rough,' Maddison agreed. 'And they mean it. They have Starky over a barrel. They know all about Laura Nolan's murder. So much in fact that they even deposited her dress in Starky's closet. They have Starky on a suspicion of murder which they can drop either way, and his daughter is in their hands. If Starky doesn't co-operate, it's curtains.'

'And what does Starky do?'

'If Mary Lewis had not been present he might have played right into their hands. As it was, she persuaded him to do otherwise. He's putting on a brave front. It's out of his hands now.'

'Why didn't you tell me this yesterday?' Hugan growled.

'Starky was warned that if he made one move towards telling the authorities, or the police, they would know about it immediately and his family would suffer.'

'So you tried me out yesterday,' Hugan growled.

'I took a gamble that if they weren't bluffing you were not their man.'

'Thanks for nothing,' Hugan said scowling.

'Look, Hugan what else could I do? You know what would happen. You would tap his phone and put a twenty-four hour tail on him. You couldn't help yourself. The opposition would smell it a mile away.'

'O.K.,' Hugan said. 'You've made your point. What do we do?'

'You do absolutely nothing to spoil the pitch.'

'Look, I got a Police Chief,' Hugan said aggressively.

'I know. You continue with your investigations as normal. I'll keep you posted.'

Hugan didn't like it. He didn't like being dictated to by a young, raw, Federal man, but he had no alternative.

'Anything else?' he asked.

'There was a call from the cabbie who drove Starky back to his bungalow,' Maddison said. 'They've been keeping him low.'

'Very low,' Hugan said.

'He phoned Starky at the Country Club last night, round about 10 p.m. Said Starky was in trouble. Offered to tell him about it for three hundred dollars.'

'You overheard this?'

'Part of it. It was genuine. He said that he would contact Starky early this morning to give him the arrangements of the meeting.'

'Has he phoned?'

'No,' Maddison said.

'Why?' Hugan asked. 'What do you think it is all about?'

'I think Starky is being softened for the touch by somebody or some people, to make him get hold of some secret information. I also think that someone close to Starky – possibly someone at the Research Centre knows how important the information is. How vital it is to the Russians. If that is the case, that someone is possibly keeping a tight watch on Starky and on his accomplices. If, whoever it is got wind of the call last night, then they would make damn sure it wasn't repeated.'

'You think there is a corpse somewhere?'

'Yeah.'

Hugan looked thoughtful.

'If someone is already close enough to Cusack's results why don't they just take what they can and make a run for it? Or, alternatively, wait until the heat is off?'

'Yeah, they could,' Maddison agreed, 'but it would be like giving up a rich oil well. If they can make Starky do it all for them, then they can kill two birds with one stone. Besides, perhaps they aren't that close.'

'Meaning?'

Maddison shrugged. 'Could be somebody on the fringe. Somebody who knows the deadline and has a shrewd idea of what gives, but is not actually involved.'

'Like Hendrich?'

'Like Hendrich,' Maddison agreed, 'but it is a very wide field. There is all the staff at the Centre and McIntyre's crew.'

'Yeah. It is a wide field. You working on them?'

'We're back checking,' Maddison said. 'Starky has been identified in Philadelphia.'

'Yeah, he's known there,' Hugan growled. 'When is the deadline?'

'Next Friday,' Maddison replied. 'Then it becomes Washington's responsibility and Senator Leebright's in particular.'

'Could that be significant?' Hugan asked.

'Perhaps,' Maddison replied, 'but the action is taking place right here, with Starky.'

'What about Starky?' Hugan asked seriously.

Maddison looked equally serious.

'He's a frightened man,' he said grimly. 'I'll admit he worries me because I don't know whether he'll go through with it. I'll also admit that I wondered a long time about that phone call just happening to take place when Mary Lewis was with him.'

'Yeah, it would worry me,' Hugan growled.

'Anything on Laura Nolan?' Maddison asked.

'We found a note book, pocket size. In it she had a string of names and a bit of history about each.'

'Who was on her list?'

'Logan, Kay, Ludvick, Cusack, Starky, McIntyre, Benson, Hendrich, Rishman, Liefman, Botelli, Anderson.'

'Who are the last four?'

'Two are on McIntyre's staff. The other

two work at the plant.'

'Blackmail?' Maddison asked grimly.

'That is the way it looks,' Hugan replied.

'Anything else on her?'

'She received a telephone call last Wednesday. She used to get regular calls – long distance. This one didn't surprise her. I reckon it was from the same source as before.'

'Man or woman?'

'Laura Nolan's landlady didn't know. She assumed it was a man. Laura Nolan changed and went out at 7.45 p.m. She drove to the Country Club which again points to someone on her list. Ninety per cent of them are members. Let us assume she parks her car in the park. No one has yet come forward to say that they saw her, but we have two testimonies that the car was there at 8 p.m. She then walked to her meeting.'

'Nobody see her?'

'Not her, but one of the keepers from the Club has a house near the river bank. He reckons he saw a car come out of the turning close to the wood about eight-fifteen as he was walking home. All he saw was the car and a figure of a man driving it, hunched up over the wheel.'

'What was he wearing?'

'A trilby and light suit.'

'The same type of car as Starky's?' Maddison asked.

'Could be,' Hugan said, 'but they are all alike to this guy, and it was dark, don't forget.'

'And you feel this was the killer?'

'We searched the spot; it could have been the place of the murder.'

'Find anything?'

'Nothing to pin it down. There was evidence of people having been there before. Broken foliage, etcetera, but nothing that would point to the murder.'

'So what are you working on now?'

'We were looking for her clothes, but according to your evidence the murderer has them.'

'So it would seem. How about the cars?'

'We've run the rule over everybody's car who knew Laura Nolan.'

'And?'

'The keeper's description of the car could fit one of a hundred,' Hugan growled, 'and by the time we got to them they could have all been stripped clean.'

'How about the timing angle,' Maddison asked. 'Could Starky have got from the Club to Luigi's?'

'He could,' Hugan said sourly. 'He reckons

he got there about eight o'clock, but he could be lying.'

'But he couldn't have driven to his bungalow, deposited the body in his bedroom, and driven back to the parking lot at the back of the Central Garage,' Maddison said.

'No,' Hugan agreed reluctantly. 'It takes twenty minutes from the Club to Riverside and twenty from Riverside to the Central Garage. The attendant swears he would have seen Starky park his car on the lot after 8 p.m. That car got there between 7.30 p.m. and 8 p.m.'

'So if Starky is your man at the Country Club, how did he get the body back to his bungalow?'

'He either had an accomplice,' Hugan snapped, 'or Laura Nolan was murdered elsewhere.'

'Accomplice?' Maddison asked.

'Yeah, why not?' Hugan retorted.

'Yeah, why not?' Maddison agreed, but didn't sound convinced. He fastened his necktie and put on his jacket. At the same moment, the lieutenant's wife burst through the doorway.

'Oh!' she said in surprise. 'I didn't know you were expected.'

She was wearing a flowered silk dress and

white straw hat. It was her regular outfit in the summer, for church.

'I called unexpectedly,' Maddison smiled.

Hugan watched his wife. He wished Maddison had left before she had returned.

'Won't you stay for lunch?' Mrs Hugan asked. The lieutenant's mouth fell open in surprise.

'That's very kind of you,' Maddison said, 'very kind, but unfortunately I have made arrangements.'

'Then you must come for supper one evening.'

The lieutenant stood speechless and annoyed. Speechless at his wife's sudden burst of hospitality and annoyed that it was directed at Maddison. She had never had any of his friends from the department for supper. Why Maddison?

'Certainly, Mrs Hugan. I would really like to.'

'Good,' Mrs Hugan beamed. 'Now which evening is going to suit you two the best?'

The lieutenant found his voice.

'That depends, Madge,' he said firmly. 'Doesn't it, Maddison?' He didn't give Maddison time to reply. 'I will tie it up with Maddison and let you know, dear. Probably later in the week.'

'All right, John.'

Maddison got the feeling that if it was left to the lieutenant he wouldn't be around.

'I'll hold him to it,' he said to Mrs Hugan.

He crossed over to the doorway. 'That is a pretty dress,' he said, smiling. 'My favourite colours.'

'Oh!' Mrs Hugan's eyes lit up. 'Thank you.'

The lieutenant opened the kitchen door.

'Good-bye Maddison,' he said pointedly. 'You know how to contact me.'

Maddison looked at the lieutenant.

'I think you would suit blue, lieutenant,' he said with an air of mischievousness. 'Match your eyes.'

Before the lieutenant had time to give a caustic retort, Maddison had left him standing.

'The young whippersnapper,' the lieutenant growled. He went back into the kitchen. From the adjoining room came the sound of his wife singing. The lieutenant raised his eyebrows and nodded his head approvingly. 'Well, what do you know?' he said aloud to himself. He hadn't heard Madge singing like that as she did the housework since they had received the telegram. Perhaps he should have Maddison to supper after all.

Like Starky's, Jayson Hendrich's Sunday looked as if it wasn't going to go according to plan. From the outset he also had the feeling that it was going to be one of those off-days. He had been late to bed. After leaving the Club the previous evening he had dropped his wife off at their house on the pretext of having an hour's game of poker with some of his employees at a bar in town. Instead he had gone to Ma Holling's establishment and spent a couple of hours with one of her girls. The thought of those two hours only just compensated for the thick head he carried down to the breakfast table.

Silently he picked up the newspaper. Emily was dressed. She had breakfasted earlier.

'I thought we might take a run up to the lodge, Jayson,' she said.

'Ugh?' Hendrich looked at his wife from over the top of the newspaper and scowled. 'What the hell for?'

'Well, we haven't been up there for a while. Goodness knows what it is like.'

Hendrich had no desire to go to the lodge – at least not with Emily. He had got it on the pretext that they could weekend in the country. He had wanted it as a symbol of his

135

success. Occasionally he would take some of the boys from the plant up for a weekend's shooting and drinking. Rarely he took Emily. He found it too boring and he was not a nature boy.

'No thanks,' he growled. 'Not for me. Go yourself if you must.'

Emily sighed. She had long since stopped being hurt by her husband's lack of interest. She suspected his infidelity. The whole business upset her not because of a personal jealousy, but because of a feeling of frustration and waste. There was only one life. They both deserved to have the comfort of another person. Neither was getting it and occasionally it hurt. This was one of the mornings when she felt it.

'What are you going to do?' she asked.

Hendrich frowned. Why the hell couldn't she just leave him alone?

'I think I'll take a flip,' he said in a tone that didn't invite discussion.

He went to Jackson Field, but found no one to join him. He went flying by himself, which he didn't like, returned to the Field sooner than he had intended. On his way home he called in at the Red Barn Tavern and had a few beers. That didn't make him feel any happier. When he reached his driveway he was feeling thoroughly flat and bad tempered. When he drove up to the car port the feeling became one of nervousness. Standing in his driveway was a police car!

Hendrich parked his car. He saw Emily at the entrance porch with two detectives. Hendrich had talked to one of them before about Laura Nolan. The detectives came up to him.

'Good afternoon, Mr Hendrich,' one of them said. 'I understand that you have been to Jackson Field.'

'Yeah,' Hendrich said. He felt a foreboding. 'What gives?'

'Lieutenant Hugan would like you to come to Railton,' the detective said calmly.

'Railton?' Hendrich asked. 'What the hell for?'

'He will tell you, Mr Hendrich.'

'Well, he can come here and tell me,' Hendrich said sharply. He saw the look of concern on his wife's face. What the hell was worrying her? he wondered.

'You do own a lodge at Pine Creek in Railton?' the detective asked patiently.

'Yeah,' Hendrich agreed.

'In that case, I think you had better come with us,' the detective said. Hendrich looked at him. There was an air of determination on the detective's face. His companion moved fractionally towards Hendrich as if he were going to hustle him into the police car.

'O.K.' Hendrich growled. 'O.K.' He looked at his wife and saw the look on her face again. She was genuinely worried, he thought. Hell, what do you know? She was actually concerned about him. He got into the police car. The detectives got in beside him. Hendrich wondered what the lieutenant was after. Why drag him all the way up to the lodge? Railton was out of the lieutenant's jurisdiction. It was the Sheriff's territory. He didn't question the detectives. In fact they hardly spoke. Just sat like two stuffed mutes. Hendrich tried to talk to them. They just shut him up. It made him feel worse. Like a criminal.

When they got to Railton they drove straight to the lodge at Pine Creek. Two other police cars were parked along the track and a number of the Sheriff's men stood about. The detectives ushered Hendrich out of the car. A burly sergeant of the Sheriff's County Police appeared from nowhere.

'This is your place?' he asked flatly. He had a deadpan face which gave nothing away and a voice that matched it.

'Yeah,' Hendrich agreed. 'What's it all about?'

'When did you last visit it?' the sergeant asked.

'Hell, I can't remember. Last month, I think.'

'Did you let it out to anyone recently?'

'No,' Hendrich said firmly.

'Then you wouldn't be expecting anybody to be living here?'

'Hell no, why should they?'

'Somebody has been living here,' the sergeant said acidly, 'and that someone is inside.'

There was more to come, Hendrich thought. They hadn't dragged him all the way to the lodge just to tell him that. From the corner of his eye he saw Lieutenant Hugan watching him. They had met before when the lieutenant had been at the plant asking about Laura Nolan. Hendrich didn't like the look on his face.

'That someone is dead,' the sergeant added. 'Shot in the side of the face with a shot gun.'

Hendrich's face went pale.

'Do you have a shot gun?' the sergeant asked.

'Yeah,' Hendrich said quietly. 'I keep it in the lodge.'

'Find it,' the sergeant said and nodded his

head to one of his uniformed deputies, 'and when you are inside, see if you can recognise the body.'

The deputy took Hendrich's arm and led him up the steps and into the lodge. A flash bulb exploded making Hendrich start. He saw a body on the floor and the group of police standing around it. They moved as he came closer and he saw the bloody mess where there had once been a face. He felt his stomach turn over. The sergeant came up to him.

'Do you recognise the clothing or any part of him?' he asked.

Hendrich forced himself to look again at the body on the floor. It was being lifted on to a stretcher. He saw a checked shirt and a pair of brown pants, and kept his eyes away from the bloody mess of the face.

'No,' he said hoarsely. 'No.'

He saw Burt Raker, who lived the whole year round in the lodge by the river, sitting in a corner beside a uniformed deputy. Raker smiled weakly at him.

'Hi, Mr Hendrich,' Raker called across to him. Raker stood up as if to come over to Hendrich, but the deputy got in the way. Hendrich didn't see what happened, but Raker sat down again. Hendrich felt sorry for him and wondered why the hell he had been dragged into the net.

'Where's the gun?' the sergeant asked grimly.

Hendrich went to the cupboard where he always kept it and opened the door. There was no gun!

'It's gone!' he exclaimed.

'Yeah,' the sergeant agreed. 'It's not here. We've looked.'

A deputy took Hendrich to the veranda. 'Wait here,' he ordered. Hendrich stood and stared vacantly at the headlamps of the police cars.

He saw the sergeant and Lieutenant Hugan deep in conversation. With the lieutenant were the two plain clothed detectives who had brought Hendrich to the lodge. The sergeant and the lieutenant came up to him.

'You don't recognise anything about him?' the sergeant asked again.

Hendrich shook his head.

'Any idea why he might be in the lodge?'

Again Hendrich shook his head. 'None at all,' he said.

'When were you last here?'

'About a month or so ago.'

'Why did your wife phone Raker to check the place out?'

Hendrich looked up at the sergeant. So Emily had phoned Raker, and he had come over to the lodge and found the body.

'She probably wanted to make sure everything was O.K.,' he said hesitantly.

'Does she normally worry about the place after a month?' the sergeant asked flatly.

'Yeah,' Hendrich lied and wondered why the hell Emily had bothered Raker. She had never done it before. 'She's like that,' he added. 'Worries a lot.'

'But she has never phoned Raker before and asked him to check it out,' the sergeant persisted.

'No,' Hendrich agreed sadly.

'Then why did she do it this time?'

How the hell should I know, Hendrich thought. He and Emily hardly ever spoke, never mind discuss anything.

'She got an idea about coming to the lodge today to check it out herself. When she learned I was going to the Field…'

'Jackson Field?' the sergeant interrupted.

'Yeah, I fly.'

'Go on.'

'Well, she must have gotten a fixation about the place. She often does.'

'So she phoned Raker to come over and have a look?'

'Yeah.'

The sergeant looked grim faced. Hendrich had a feeling that he didn't accept his explanation. He began to feel anxious.

'Would you mind coming to the station?' the sergeant asked.

'What the hell for?' Hendrich demanded.

'Just to answer a few further questions,' the sergeant said patiently. Another burly figure in uniform appeared alongside Hendrich.

'You are going to be co-operative, aren't you?' the figure asked. Hendrich got the message.

'Sure,' he said. 'I've got nothing to hide.' But he wondered what Emily had said about his trip into town after they had left the Country Club the previous evening. The stiff in the lodge looked as if he had been dead a long time. If the cops wanted to know where Hendrich had been during the night it could be awkward. He didn't want people to know that he had been with one of the broads. Hell! No. It would finish him. A cold sweat came over him. God! If it ever came out that he had been with one of Ma Holling's girls he would be ruined. A wave of panic gripped his bowels. His legs felt weak. Hendrich began to sweat as Starky

143

had sweated, but for a different reason.

As Hendrich was being taken away, one of the detectives went up to Hugan.

'I wonder who the dame is that stiff has been phoning regularly?' the detective asked.

'Probably some broad that he had waiting for him,' Hugan growled.

'Could be,' the detective sighed. 'Do you think there is a link with the Nolan case?'

'Yeah,' Hugan said, but said no more. He didn't tell his assistant what Maddison had told him that morning, or that a man answering the description of the dead man had also made a telephone call last night from the roadhouse in Pine Creek at the same time that Maddison had told him Starky had been contacted. It was also too much of a coincidence that Jayson Hendrich should get a mention in Laura Nolan's diary. There had to be a link somewhere.

'I want to know the exact time of death,' he said, 'and then get on to Starky and see what his alibi is.' He still had the feeling about Starky. 'I'm going to the Station and have a long talk with Hendrich when the sergeant is through with him.'

A uniformed deputy came up to him.

'There's a character over there wants a

word with you, Lieutenant,' he said. 'Reckons he's a friend of yours.'

Hugan looked into the darkness and saw a figure step in front of a car headlamp. It was a slim, bearded man with a pipe in his mouth and a rifle slung over his shoulder. He was wearing rough, hunting clothes. The lieutenant reluctantly walked over to him. He would have preferred to have given the man a miss. Not because of any personal dislike of the man, but because the man brought back painful memories. The man was Jake Cullen, locally called Beaver. He was the best woodsman, fisherman, and hunter in the northern territory. Hugan had used his expertise often in the past.

'Howdy, Lieutenant,' Beaver said in his broad country accent.

'Hullo, Beaver,' Hugan replied. He held out his hand. Beaver shook it warmly.

'Long time since you been in these parts,' Beaver said.

'Yeah,' Hugan agreed.

'Sorry to hear about your boy, Lieutenant.'

'What brings you down here, Beaver?' Hugan asked, deliberately changing the subject. 'Thought you spent all your evenings in the Tavern.'

'Sure do,' Beaver smiled. 'Came down to see the sergeant.'

'About that business?' Hugan asked, indicating the lodge.

'Nope.' Beaver spat out some chew. 'Never laid eyes on him. Been over the south side mostly. Came to make a complaint.'

'Complaint?'

'Some critter landed his plane over in the south west corner of the lake. Came in very early one morning last week. Made a mess of some of my nets.'

'Times are changing, Beaver,' Hugan said. 'Besides they are good for business.'

'That's true, Lieutenant, but they're supposed to use the stretch of water north of the flats. That critter has frightened away those ducks for ever.'

'They'll be back,' Hugan said and slapped the man affectionately on the shoulder.

'I'm not so sure,' Beaver persisted. 'If I ever get my hands on him…'

'Sure, Beaver,' Hugan didn't want to pursue the matter. 'I'll report it to the sergeant. I'm going to the Station.'

'Thanks, Lieutenant.'

'See you some time, Beaver.'

'Sure. Give my regards to your missus. Sure was sorry to hear about your boy.'

Hugan turned and walked away.

'Come up some time, Lieutenant,' Beaver called out. 'We'll go fishing again.'

Hugan acknowledged the remark with a wave of his hand. Perhaps he would, he thought, and then felt a dull ache inside of him. No, he wouldn't. There were too many memories.

NINE

When Lieutenant Hugan left Railton the Sheriff's men were still making Hendrich sweat. Hugan suggested to the sergeant that Starky might be able to help, but Hugan didn't want to be around when they pulled him in. Already the sergeant was asking Hugan questions that he was finding difficult to answer. Starky wouldn't make it any easier, but the lieutenant wanted him to identify the stiff from the lodge. He left two of his detectives to work with the sheriff's men and drove back to Medway Springs. After a quick visit to Headquarters he returned to his home and found Maddison, sitting in his car, waiting for him.

Hugan went up to him.

'Can't it wait until the morning?' he growled. 'Even cops are entitled to sleep.'

'Not this one,' Maddison replied evenly. 'My chief wants to see you.'

'Council of war?'

'Something like that,' Maddison agreed and opened his passenger door. 'Do you mind coming with me?'

'Yeah, I do,' Hugan said and meant it, but he got into the car.

Maddison smiled to himself at the lieutenant's manner and didn't try to antagonise him any further. He quickly drove the lieutenant to a ranchhouse about ten miles out of town where Weiderman was waiting for them.

Inside the house Hugan didn't try to hide his displeasure. He was beginning to feel that he was no longer in control of his investigations and it was a feeling that he didn't like.

Weiderman sensed the lieutenant's feelings and realised that the only way of winning him over was to be constructive. After introducing his assistant, Vasey, and the other agents, he got down to business.

'Something important has turned up,' he said.

The lieutenant and Maddison looked at him.

'Last week the Department got a request for Starky to be given a green pass,' Weiderman explained.

'Green pass?' Hugan asked.

'At the plant there are three different grades of security. A green pass entitles the bearer to have access to the research laboratory and all its records. The only people who have it at present are the four scientists, Dr Logan, and McIntyre. The rest of the unit have either a yellow pass or a red pass which entitles them to certain privileges, but never to be alone, or unescorted, in the lab.'

'Laura Nolan have one?' Hugan asked.

'Yellow,' Weiderman replied. 'She was never permitted to be there alone.'

'So a green pass would give Starky a clear field to photograph any secret information,' Maddison said.

'Quite,' Weiderman agreed.

'On what grounds can they justify such a pass?' Hugan asked.

Weiderman lit a cigarette, offered his packet around the table, and blew the smoke into the room.

'The Cusack project is in its final stages,' he said. 'Next month the unit is starting work on another project. The estimates have to be into the Treasury before the end of the month. Ludvick and Kay are working on them. Starky is responsible for collecting and submitting the estimates. It is a long job. Needs close co-operation between those who are going to be involved and the accountancy side. The report is classified so

151

it would seem logical that the three men get together in the security wing.'

'Who made the request?' Maddison asked.

'Dr Logan,' Weiderman replied, 'with McIntyre's approval.'

'Who initiated it?' Hugan growled.

Weiderman shrugged.

'A good point, Lieutenant,' he said, 'but that is the hundred dollar question. Logan would have to make the request. He is the only one who could. McIntyre would have to approve it. He is security. Who started the ball rolling? Ludvick? Kay? or Starky?'

'It's wide open,' Maddison sighed. 'If we knew who started the ball rolling we might have a good idea who was pushing Starky.'

'Might?' Weiderman asked.

Maddison shrugged. 'It could be coincidental. When was the request originally submitted?'

'Logan sent it off on the thirteenth of last month.'

'Before Laura Nolan was murdered,' Maddison pointed out.

No one made any comment.

'The question is, do we go along with it?' Weiderman asked.

'Yes,' Maddison said firmly. 'We have no alternative.'

'It's a dangerous move,' Weiderman warned. 'If we lose out on it we're going to look pretty stupid.'

'It's too late now to back out,' Maddison said quietly.

Weiderman looked stern. 'Agreed,' he said.

'Starky was contacted again today,' Maddison said. 'Tomorrow he receives the hardware.'

'And the green pass,' Weiderman added.

'The next move is the take and delivery,' Vasey warned.

'The delivery is where we come in,' Weiderman said grimly.

'Not before?' Hugan asked.

'Not before,' Weiderman said, shaking his head. 'We do nothing until we know where and when the delivery is to be made.'

'And how do you get to know that?' Hugan growled.

'I'm going to put a tap on all calls in and out of the Riverside Estate,' Weiderman said. Both Maddison and Hugan looked surprised. 'The overhead wires from the estate join the main system at the highway by the river,' Weiderman explained, forestalling any questions. 'I'm putting two men in a trailer down there for a few days fishing. They can monitor all calls.'

'Now we're getting somewhere,' Hugan said.

'Let's see if we can get further, Lieutenant,' Weiderman said. 'Give us a quick run through your case. We might be able to fill in a few gaps.'

'Now I'm beginning to feel glad I came,' Hugan said dryly. He opened his pocket book. 'Victim: Laura Nolan,' he said. 'She leaves the plant 6 p.m. goes to her apartment, gets changed and drives to the Country Club. About 8 p.m. she is strangled, stripped, and her body eventually dumped in Harry Starky's bungalow. No one sees her arrive at the club, but in a nearby lane there are tyre marks and evidence of people having been there. A keeper reckons he heard a car engine. He also saw a car and driver pull out of the lane, but there is no conclusive evidence that the murder actually took place at this location. I've checked Nolan's background. Her parents won't say much. She spent a year in Chicago and lived with a man called Karl Lacey. So far we haven't been able to trace him.'

'Lacey was a member of the Communist Party,' Weiderman explained quietly. 'He left for South America last weekend.'

'Is that significant?' Hugan asked.

'I think so,' Weiderman replied. 'He was booked on a flight for this coming Saturday. Could be he got out of the way before we could get at him.'

'Laura Nolan a Party member?' Maddison asked.

'No evidence of her having joined the Party, but this could have been part of the plan.'

'She comes to Medway Springs prepared to help them,' Hugan said thoughtfully. 'Could explain her parents' reluctance to talk. If they knew that she was a Communist supporter that wouldn't look good with the neighbours.'

'Could be,' Weiderman agreed. 'Suppose she came to the plant working for them – go on.'

'It would explain her attitude,' Maddison said. 'She tried all the men out hoping to find a sucker for what she was after.'

'And then decided not to go through with it,' Hugan added. 'This could be the motive. She wanted out, but the Commies wouldn't play. She met her contact, told him she wasn't playing ball. She was then murdered and her body dumped in Starky's bungalow.'

'Why Starky?' Vasey asked.

''Cause everyone knew that he was out having a drink,' Hugan grumbled.

'How about your suspects?' Weiderman asked.

'Take your pick,' Hugan growled. 'I could build a case against any one of them.'

'Shoot,' someone said.

'O.K.,' Hugan said. 'Take Logan. Could be that he was being blackmailed. A couple of his trips to Chicago coincided with the times that Laura Nolan was out of town. He could have played around with her. He had good reason to. His wife and Senator Leebright were more than friendly in Washington.' He looked up at the others and saw by the looks on their faces that he was telling them nothing new. 'McIntyre gambles, drinks and plays the ponies,' he went on. 'Why? He has a nice family. Benson reckons Laura Nolan was frigid. Could be she stood him up. Kay is a ladies' man. He admits to dating Laura Nolan. Could be more to it. Ludvick is ambitious. She might have been blackmailing him. There is also the Bradley dame. She has marked sexual tendencies.'

'Meaning what?'

'She gets a regular delivery of pornographic literature from a New York firm,' Hugan said scornfully. 'The type of stuff I

156

wouldn't dirty my garbage can with.'

There was a pregnant silence. 'Anyone else?' someone asked.

'Yeah,' Hugan said. 'How about Hendrich? He is a leading light in the plant and in the community. He likes the chicks. I bet he tried it on with Laura Nolan.'

'What about alibis?' Weiderman asked.

'I could drive a horse and cart through them,' Hugan replied. 'Logan left the plant at seven p.m. and stayed in his bungalow. His wife is at the Club and it's their help's night out. Ludvick and Cusack are also in their bungalows. Ludvick's wife will vouch for him.' He scowled his displeasure. 'Kay and Helen Logan were at the Club, but Laura Nolan's car was also found there. McIntyre was at the plant all night. He has a cover except for forty minutes. Long enough for him to meet Laura Nolan. The Bradley dame was at a rehearsal at the High School and then returned to her bungalow. Hendrich reckons he was playing poker in town. The three guys he named would sell their grandmother for a quick buck. If we could find them. They're probably stoned somewhere, or out of town. As for Benson, he reckons he was in his room all night reading. Again, no one can vouch for him.'

He scowled again. 'You see my problem?'

'Yeah,' Weiderman said quietly. 'We see it.'

'And there is that stiff at Hendrich's lodge,' Hugan added.

'Starky's cab driver?' Maddison asked.

'Probably,' Hugan said. 'He was seen making a call from the Roadhouse in Pine Creek at the same time as you reckon Starky got his call.' He turned to Weiderman. 'How about you?' he asked. 'I'm looking for a murderer. What are you looking for?'

'A spy,' Weiderman said quietly, 'and that could be any one of them.' He looked grim. 'Any one of them,' he said again. He looked up at the lieutenant. 'Like you, I could build a case up for suspecting any one of them. Take their backgrounds. Cusack is Czech, Ludvick – German, Kay – British, Starky – Polish. Alternatively take a motive – Ideological – that could be Benson or any one of the scientists. Mercenary – that could be McIntyre or even the Bradley dame.' He gave a faint smile. 'You get the point?'

'We both have a problem,' Hugan growled.

'We'll solve it before the week is out,' Weiderman said confidently.

'I wish you would tell that to my chief,' Hugan retorted with feeling. 'It's going to be a long week.'

TEN

Monday, June 7th, was a stifling, hot day in Medway Springs. With the heat came the news of the second murder and a sullen atmosphere hung over the town. Questions were now being openly asked. Was there more to come? The *Morning Star* suggested a maniac was at large and urged the Chief of Police, and Sheriff to double their efforts to solve the two crimes. Although no suggestion had been made in the press of a link between the two murders, the fact that Hendrich's name was associated with the plant suggested a tie up. The press had given Hugan a fairly rough time in its Friday issue, implying that he was in a mental fog. In its Monday issue it not only hinted at a mental fog, but also at incompetence. Having missed the opportunity to headline the murder on Sunday it tried to make capital out of it on the Monday – and it succeeded.

At the Research Centre on the Monday there was a distinct atmosphere. Nothing was openly discussed, but an uneasiness existed. Harry Starky looked sullen. He had been summoned to the Sheriff's office in Railton in the late hours of the Sunday evening, taken to a room and asked to give a full description of the man who was supposed to have driven him to his bungalow from Luigi's saloon on the night of Laura Nolan's murder.

Starky had given this information before, but not to the Sheriff's men. The description he gave seemed to satisfy the sergeant who had then taken him over to the morgue to see a body. A body with part of its face mutilated, but still recognisable as his Irish cabbie! Starky later learned that he had been found dead at Hendrich's lodge in Pine Creek. After the identification came a string of questions. What time had Starky returned home the previous evening? Had he left the bungalow? The questions had lasted over an hour. Starky had then been driven back to his bungalow. He had immediately phoned Maddison only to find that he was out. That had puzzled him. It was nearly midnight. He had spoken to Maddison earlier after he had been contacted again, and Maddison had made no mention that he would not be available later. Where had he gone to? Starky wondered. Starky hadn't told the sergeant

160

about the phone call at the Club the previous evening. That was something between him and Maddison, but when Starky had looked at the body in the morgue he knew that there was now no one who could support his story... On the Monday he still had the pain at the nape of his neck...

Jayson Hendrich both fumed and sweated. His Monday started like Starky's had after Laura Nolan's body had been found in Starky's room. There was that similarity. Both men had a dead body discovered on their premises. There was another similarity. Both men gave alibis which could not be substantiated.

The time of death of the body found in Hendrich's lodge was put at 3 a.m. Hendrich had returned home after the night at the Club round about 1.30 a.m. He had dropped Emily off and driven into town, on the pretext of going for a game of poker. But he had got no further than Ma Holling's place. He had spent a couple of hours there with a coloured girl. To have admitted that would have put a noose around his neck. If the facts ever became public – the very thought sent waves of fear through his body and made him perspire profusely. Hendrich at Ma Holling's! And with a coloured girl! Hendrich suffered all that long night at the station as he sweated out his story. He had dropped off his wife, driven into town to see if he could find a game going at a couple of the bars. He had found no one there so had gone straight back home. He was back in bed by 2.30 a.m. That was his story and he was going to stick to it come hell or high water. His only worry was what Emily had told them. He knew Ma Holling would say nothing. She would charge plenty for keeping her mouth shut, but she could be relied upon. That was why some of the so-called prominent citizens used her establishment. She had built up a reputation of being tight lipped.

When Hendrich had returned home from his night in the Sheriff's office, the dawn was breaking through. As he entered the hall, Emily appeared from the kitchen in her dressing gown.

'I have some coffee on,' she said. 'I heard on the radio. Was it awful?'

'Yeah,' Hendrich growled. 'How the hell did that guy get a key to the lodge?'

He went into the kitchen and sat at the table. His wife handed him a cup of coffee.

'What did you tell them?' he asked anxiously. He gave his wife a look that she had never seen before. It was meant to intimidate her, but it didn't.

'What do you mean, Jayson?' she said calmly.

'You know damn well what I mean,' Hendrich said hotly. 'They asked you what time we returned home didn't they?'

'Yes, I told them round about 1.30 a.m.'

'What else did you tell them?'

'What else, Jayson?'

'Yeah. Look, Emily, don't play around. You told them I went out?'

'No, Jayson,' Emily Hendrich said innocently. 'Should I have?'

Hendrich stopped in the act of drinking his coffee.

'You didn't tell them?' he asked incredulously.

'They didn't ask.'

'They didn't ask!'

Hendrich sat back and gave a long, deep sigh.

'They didn't ask,' he beamed. 'Well I never.'

Emily Hendrich watched him from the stove.

'Of course,' she said quietly. 'They might get around to it.'

Hendrich swung round and saw the slim back of his wife. For once it looked straight and proud. Not bent like it had appeared before. She wouldn't, he thought. No, not Emily. He tried to throw off the thought that his wife might drop him in, but the seed was there and he recalled some of the cutting remarks he had made to her recently. And there had been that scene in the car when they had driven back from the Club. She had pleaded with him not to go into town.

Hendrich began to doubt his wife's loyalty and he began to sweat again. And he sweated all through the Monday. Whenever anyone came to him and gave him their encouragement and support, he sweated. When Pastor Douglas phoned he sweated even more.

The four scientists set about their work silently, each with their own thoughts. They worked well enough as a team because they had found a common interest – the development of their project, but that was the only reason that kept them together. On this particular Monday morning Cusack was his usual slow, ponderous, father figure; Ludvick was business-like and impatient; Kay was quiet. Only Benson wanted to talk about the newspaper reports. He tried to discuss it with Kay only to be abruptly chewed off. Kay had a sharp, cutting manner which usually didn't endear him to its recipient. On this occasion Benson was at the receiving end and he wished Kay into hell.

McIntyre sat in his office and read and re-read the newspaper reports. What the hell was going on? he wondered. Could there be any tie-up with the Laura Nolan business and the stiff at Hendrich's lodge? he wondered.

'Ah, hell,' he muttered. He was becoming unnecessarily jumpy. What tie-up could there be? The stiff was probably a hobo. Besides, the F.B.I. would have his report soon. He had sent it express. His assistant handed him a memo from Dr Logan. It was the affirmative to give Starky a green pass. Was that such a good thing at that late stage? McIntyre wondered. He stared at it long and hard before giving it his O.K.

Diana Bradley also sat in her office and read the newspaper reports closely. She had heard a car drive out of the estate during the dark and early hours of the Sunday morning. She had been sleeping badly and had got out of bed to get a stiff drink – the only sedative that seemed to help her. It was then that she had heard the car. She wondered if anyone else on the estate had heard it also.

Starky received his green pass from Dr Logan together with instructions to get the estimates tied up as soon as possible. He wasn't unduly surprised at receiving the pass, he knew that it had been put in motion. He joined Kay and Ludvick in the inner sanctuary and set about collecting the required information. He found the atmosphere in the laboratory stiff and strained. Dr Cusack and Benson were writing the report on the project and Kay and Ludvick were uncommunicative.

It was after 7 p.m. that evening when Starky returned to his bungalow. When he entered the hallway he saw a brown package on the hall table. He opened the package. Inside was a camera. He examined it closely. It had no name. It was loaded and set for action. He toyed with it thoughtfully, resisted the temptation to phone Maddison, and poured himself a stiff drink and waited.

When the phone rang it made him jump. Hesitantly he picked up the receiver. It was Hendrich.

'Harry,' Hendrich said. 'How about going out for a drink? I feel like a wet rag.'

'Sorry Jayson,' Starky said. 'I know how you feel, but I have some work to finish off.'

'Pity, Harry. Can't it wait?'

'Not this job.'

Starky could sense Hendrich's agitation. Hendrich had spoken to him at the plant and Starky had recognised the symptoms.

'Don't worry yourself, Jayson,' he said. 'It will clear itself soon.'

'What makes you so sure?'

'Just a hunch.'

'I wish you would tell that to the cops. That damned sergeant and the lieutenant won't leave me alone.'

'Likewise.'

'Sure you can't make it?'

'Some other night.'

'How about the ball game Wednesday? We could have a beer afterwards.'

'Yeah, that should be O.K.'

'See you at the plant.'

'O.K.'

Starky replaced the receiver.

Ten minutes later the phone rang again. This time it was the voice of his contact. Starky took the call, got his instructions, and afterwards phoned Maddison.

'I've just been contacted,' he said. The pain at the back of his neck began to play up again. He wished he had taken another stiff drink. 'There was a camera delivered today,' he added. 'All I have to do is take a few photographs of you know what.'

'And the pick up?' Maddison asked.

'I get my instructions later in the week,' Starky said.

'I want to know what they are immediately you get them,' Maddison said grimly.

'And what about the photographs?'

'Do nothing,' Maddison said calmly. 'Nothing.'

'Is that wise?' Starky asked. 'They have made a suggestion that there might be another victim.'

'Another victim?' Maddison asked. 'Who?'

'Mary,' Starky said quietly.

'Mary?' Maddison asked with surprise. There was a fractional pause, then he said calmly, 'I see. Never mind just do as I say. Now tell me about the camera. Describe it to me.'

Starky gave him the details. When Maddison was satisfied he rang off. Starky decided to have his stiff drink. He wondered why Maddison was so interested in the camera. He also wondered what Maddison was up to. He couldn't quite picture him just having a quiet beer on Mrs Pringle's veranda.

Starky was correct in his thinking. Maddison was not sitting contemplating their conversation. Immediately he had rung off, he got into his car and drove to the site of a caravan not very far from Starky's bungalow. The caravan which was parked by the river on Johnson's farm, close to the turn off to the Riverside Estate. Inside the caravan were two fishermen and all their fishing tackle. There was also a recording set with a line connected to the telephone link into the Riverside Estate! The two fishermen were both F.B.I. agents.

'Starky reckons he has just been contacted,' Maddison said to them. 'About thirty minutes ago.'

'Yeah,' one of the agents replied. 'We've got it on the tape.'

'Let me hear it,' Maddison said.

One of the agents transferred a tape from the recording unit to another machine. He found the start of Starky's conversation. Maddison listened intently as he heard Starky say, 'Starky speaking.'

'You got the package?' a voice asked.

'Yeah! I got it,' Starky said grimly.

'All you have to do is take a few photographs,' the voice said. 'You have Katrina to think about and possibly another victim.'

'Another victim?' Starky asked.

'Two, three, four, what does it matter?' the voice asked. 'Your girl friend is beginning to irritate me.'

'My God!' Starky exclaimed.

'You will receive further instructions during the week,' the voice continued. 'I will know when you have the goods. After that you will be directed.'

The line went dead: the call was finished. The agent stopped the tape.

'He had an earlier conversation with Hendrich,' he explained, 'about a ball game. It is all on the tape.'

'He was telling the truth,' the other agent remarked.

'Yeah,' Maddison sighed. 'He is getting his calls all right and that means there is someone making them.' He looked at the two agents hopefully. 'Can you tell me if the call came from outside the estate or from someone on the estate?'

Both agents shook their head.

'Sorry, Gary,' one of them said. 'We can't tell.'

'I thought not,' Maddison said quietly. 'Let me have the tape. I'll take it to Vasey and let him run through it. We might get a lead from it.'

'What's the next move?' one of the men asked.

'The camera switch,' Maddison replied thoughtfully. 'Now that we know the type he has, we must change it for one of our specials.'

Maddison was worried. He suspected a new twist was about to be brought into play. The threat of another killing had been unexpected, and the possibility of the victim being Mary was getting too close to home.

'Record all calls,' he added grimly. 'I'll arrange for the next tape to be collected in the morning.'

'Hang on, Gary,' one of the agents said. 'Here's another call.'

He held up a pair of headphones and the three men listened to a conversation between Hendrich and McIntyre.

'He's getting a party together for a ball game,' one of the men said. 'Seems a sociable sort of guy, doesn't he?'

'Very,' Maddison agreed thoughtfully. 'Very.'

ELEVEN

It was still stifling hot on the Tuesday, and to add to the discomfort of those connected with the two crimes came a fresh barrage of cross-examinations and inspections. Starky's bungalow, and those of his neighbours on the small estate, was taken apart. At the plant an army of detectives questioned all and sundry.

Starky had the ache in the nape of his neck which throbbed away all day. He worked in the laboratory alongside Kay, but even if Starky had wanted to photograph any of Cusack's reports the opportunity never presented itself.

Wednesday was a little cooler. Starky had got some drugs from the plant doctor to kill the pain and hoped for a better day. The doctor said it was caused through tension. Starky thought how right he was.

In the evening everything in the town closed down for the local ball game. Hendrich had got tickets and gathered a party around him. Starky was included, but before he left for the ground, he was again contacted. This time his contact was more aggressive and threatening. Starky was to photograph the necessary papers by Friday or there would be another murder. Starky, tense and on edge, reported the message to Maddison who had already been informed by the agents in the caravan. Maddison told Starky to relax and enjoy the ball game. Starky gave verbal vent to his feelings and went to the game. So did Maddison, Hugan and several other pairs of watchful eyes. Diana Bradley went to her rehearsal in town and one of the agents from the caravan went to Starky's bungalow and replaced the camera with one of the Department's specials.

After the game Starky went to Hendrich's house for a get together. An F.B.I. car kept watch on the house and Maddison joined Lieutenant Hugan on his porch. The lieutenant was becoming less antagonistic towards the younger F.B.I. man and was beginning to like having him around, although he would never have admitted it openly.

The lieutenant handed Maddison a can of beer and flung a newspaper on to the table.

'I see Senator Leebright is making a name

for himself in St Paul,' he said.

On the front page was the Senator's photograph.

'Minneapolis tomorrow,' Maddison sighed, 'and Medway Springs, Friday.'

'In for the kill, eh?' Hugan growled.

'Or the pickings up afterwards,' Maddison said. 'If we foul it up, he'll go to town.'

'Yeah, he's an all-time winner,' Hugan said. 'Whichever way it falls, he'll make the front page out of it.' He toyed with his glass. 'You know the Senator's a lucky man.'

'How come?' Maddison asked.

'Supposing that Russian hadn't defected to the West,' Hugan explained. 'We would know nothing about the set up.'

'And?'

'When the leak became eventually known, who was going to look stupid?'

'The Senator,' Maddison agreed. 'It's been his baby from the start.' He took a drink of his beer. 'But the Senator would ride it. He's a clever cooky.'

'Sure,' Hugan agreed, 'but it would bring him down a peg or two.'

'What are you driving at?' Maddison asked earnestly.

'Who would like to see the Senator's star dimmed?' Hugan asked.

'There are a million,' Maddison said grimly.

'And one in particular,' Hugan persisted. 'Logan.'

'Dr Logan?' Maddison asked sharply.

'Sure, why not? The Senator had an affair with Logan's wife. Isn't that good enough reason for revenge?'

'And Logan is in a position to know everything about the project,' Maddison added thoughtfully.

'And he was in an accessible position in Washington to be contacted by a Russian agent.'

'O.K.,' Maddison said. 'You made a good point. We have a suspect, Logan, but there are others.'

'Go ahead, shoot,' Hugan said.

'Dr Cusack,' Maddison said grimly. 'He has been a regular attender at all international scientific conferences since he joined Columbia University.' He took a drink of his beer. 'And there are the others just as Weiderman explained.'

The lieutenant opened his mouth to make comment, but changed his mind. Madge had swung the car into the driveway. She was having a fussy time parking it. She always did, Hugan thought. She drove the car as if it was going to run away with her. He muttered something to himself.

'Mrs Hugan has arrived,' Maddison smiled.

'Yeah,' Hugan said thoughtfully and began to wonder.

Madge Hugan slammed the car door and came on to the porch. Maddison stood up.

'Why hello, Mr Maddison,' she smiled.

'Good evening, Mrs Hugan,' Maddison replied. 'Please call me Gary.'

'Gary,' Madge Hugan repeated the name. 'A nice name.' She turned to her husband. 'Would you get me a drink dear?' she asked.

'Certainly.' Hugan was only too pleased to see his wife in a sociable mood again. He went into the kitchen and took his time about getting Madge's drink. He knew that she liked Maddison, and Maddison seemed to be good for her. He mixed her one of her fruity favourites with all the trimmings. When he went back to the porch, his wife turned to him.

'John,' she said forcibly, 'fetch me down Daniel's photograph from the bedroom.'

Hugan froze. He could feel his inside churn over.

'Gary has been asking me about him, and I would like to show him that photograph.'

A hard, cold look came over Hugan's face.

What right had Maddison to question her about Danny, their Danny? Why, the young whippersnapper

'And while you are about it, John,' Madge continued, 'fetch the album.'

Hugan looked hard at Maddison. Maddison returned the look regretfully, but unashamedly.

'Now, John, are you going to do it, or do I?' Madge demanded hotly. She stood up and looked defiantly into her husband's face. Their eyes met. They had been married forty years, they had rarely quarrelled. Madge had been very difficult since their son had been killed. So had Hugan, but they had avoided open defiance of each other. Hugan looked into his wife's hazel eyes. He saw them melt into sympathetic tenderness.

'Please, John,' she said. 'I want you to.' She touched his hand and took the glass from him. 'Why, you have mixed me my favourite drink.' She turned to Maddison. 'He only does this as a rule when he's out to win me over or wants something.' She turned back to her husband. 'Now I want something John.'

Hugan knew that he was at a crossroad. If he defied his wife now she would never forgive him. Their love for each other would never be the same. He dropped his eyes and turned away. With a heavy heart he walked back into the living room. Madge had never spoken about Daniel to anyone not since that night they had received the telegram. Daniel! He felt like running to his bedroom and shutting the world behind him – but he didn't. He had always told his son to face everything as it came, with head high – never shirk. He went to the bedroom, collected the picture of their son and got the album from the bureau.

'This is Daniel,' Madge said proudly showing the photograph of their son in an officer's uniform. Maddison accepted the photograph.

'He was a fine looking boy, Mrs Hugan,' Maddison said tenderly. 'A really fine looking boy and he has your eyes.'

'Yes, everyone said that,' Madge agreed.

'But your husband's stubborn chin.'

'Right again,' Madge laughed. 'Oh! he could be stubborn all right. Remember that night when he refused to go and apologise to Else Mitchell's boy? Remember, John?'

'Yes, I remember,' Hugan said sadly.

'Oh, he was a fine boy, Gary,' Madge said longingly. 'He was going to be an engineer. He would have made a fine one too. He had passed all his exams.'

Hugan sat back and his mind went back to those years when they had been a family. He heard his wife telling of the boy's youth, his days at High School and College. How he had been drafted into the Army and how proud they had been when they had gone to see him pass out of officer school. They had had to do without their summer holiday for that trip, but it had been worth it.

Hugan listened and his heart melted. Even when his wife recalled the telegram telling them of how their son had been killed in Vietnam in the spring of 1969, she made it sound so honourable and touching.

Madge talked and talked – Maddison listened. The only time he interrupted her was when she showed him a photograph of Daniel when he was a baby, with Hugan and some of his former contemporaries.

'That's John,' she said when Maddison had asked. 'The man holding Daniel is Sergeant Shean.'

'I wouldn't have recognised you, Lieutenant,' Maddison said seriously.

'People change in the years,' Hugan replied. 'That was taken when Daniel was two years old. That's a long time back.'

'Yes,' Maddison replied thoughtfully,

'people do change.'

'Now here is one of Daniel and John later the same year.'

Madge Hugan relived her son's life well into the night. At the end Hugan had to stop her.

'Gary has a long day ahead of him tomorrow,' he said, and was surprised he had called Maddison by his Christian name.

'Thank you, Gary,' Madge Hugan said, touching his hand. 'I have needed that for a long time.'

'Sure.'

'I'll see you to the car,' Hugan said.

The two men left the porch. Neither spoke. Words would have been difficult. At the roadway Maddison said, 'I'll call you at the office.'

'O.K.' was all that Hugan said.

As Maddison drove off Hugan returned to his wife who was still sitting on the porch. She looked up at him and smiled serenely.

'Madge,' Hugan said hoarsely, 'that's the first time you have talked about Danny since...'

'Yes,' Madge Hugan replied gently, 'but nobody has ever asked me to before.'

'But I thought you didn't...' Hugan's voice trailed away. He lifted his wife out of her chair and wrapped his arms around her. 'Oh! Madge,' he whispered. 'I've wanted to talk about Danny just like we did tonight over and over again, but I was frightened it would hurt you.'

'Funny how two people can live together and not really know what the other person is thinking,' Madge said. 'I thought it was you who would be hurt.'

'Oh! Madge,' Hugan said. 'All this time...'

They stood together closer in body and spirit than they had ever been before.

TWELVE

On the Thursday Starky spent a busy, but frustrating day working with Kay in the laboratory. Cusack was in his office writing his final report. Ludvick and Benson were busy elsewhere in the lab. There was little conversation. Only when Kay required further information did Ludvick or Benson join Starky. At lunch time Starky returned to his own office to work on the information he had collected. Soon his work with Kay would be finished. It would also be the close of the present project. It was common knowledge that Senator Leebright was visiting them the following day to be informed of the project report. This pending visit by the Senator seemed to hang over the Research Centre like an executioner's axe. The Senator had that effect on people.

At the end of the day Starky had been given no opportunity to get access to any aspects of Cusack's report even if his heart had been set on doing so. In the evening he refused an invitation by Logan to make up a fourth at bridge, or to join Hendrich in a poker game. Instead he remained in his bungalow and drank more than the required amount of rye to get him into the same happier and more relaxed state of mind that he had felt on the night of his birthday. He finally staggered to his bed in a semi-drunken stupor.

Whilst Starky found his day uneventful, Maddison found it very rewarding. In the afternoon Weiderman returned from a meeting with Senator Leebright in St Paul and summoned Maddison to his headquarters at the ranch. Immediately Maddison met the chief, he realised there had been a break through.

'Something turn up?' he asked.

'Yes,' Weiderman replied. 'McIntyre.'

'McIntyre?' Maddison exclaimed.

'Here is a report which he sent to the Bureau in Washington last Sunday.'

Maddison accepted the report and read through it carefully. It was an appraisal of all the staff and of the events over the past few months. It was a good report and urged the Bureau to act immediately. When Maddison had read it he and Weiderman looked solemnly at each other. There was no one else in the room.

'How far can we trust him?' Maddison asked. 'It could be a blind.'

'Think so?'

Maddison shook his head. He and Weiderman both had a shrewd idea who their man was.

'McIntyre asks for a member of the department to contact him,' Weiderman said. 'We could use some help.'

'Yeah,' Maddison said thoughtfully.

'I'll send Vasey,' Weiderman said. 'We'll play it very careful.'

'What about the Senator?' Maddison asked. 'We don't want to upset him.'

'True,' Weiderman agreed grimly. 'His caravan arrives in town tomorrow. He is due at the Research Centre in the afternoon.'

'In for the kill?'

'Yeah. One way or another Medway Springs is going to become a household name. The Senator will see to that.'

'What do we tell him?' Maddison asked.

'About Starky?' Weiderman asked.

'And the camera switch?' Maddison added.

'We'll tell him about Starky and the camera switch,' Weiderman said solemnly. 'But not McIntyre or anyone else. Those who do know we can trust.'

The two men exchanged glances.

'Let's hope nothing goes wrong,' Maddison sighed. 'The Senator can make a lot of noise.'

'Don't worry,' Weiderman said encouragingly. 'I'm convinced we know who our man is.'

'So am I,' Maddison smiled. More so than ever, he thought, after his talk with Hugan the previous evening and now McIntyre's report. 'Any reply to those queries yet?'

'Not yet,' Weiderman said. 'I'll contact you as soon as they come in.'

'O.K.,' Maddison replied. 'There is nothing to do but wait for the big day.'

'Starky's big day,' Weiderman said thoughtfully.

'It's everybody's,' Maddison added seriously. 'But it all hinges around Starky.'

'Let's hope he doesn't let us down.'

'Or have a hangover,' Maddison added. 'I have a feeling he will be consoling himself this evening with a bottle.'

As it turned out Starky didn't have a hangover or throbbing pain the following day, which was a great surprise and relief to him. He set about his breakfast and his daily chores with even a light heart. He heard the mail arrive and wondered what to expect. There were a couple of bills which he read with unusual interest. As he left the bungalow, he got a strange feeling that he was being watched. He couldn't put his finger on it, but he felt it. Someone, somewhere, was watching him. In the middle of the rear seat of his car was a square paper box about eight inches cube. He picked it up and wondered when it had been put there. He slowly opened it. The lid flew off and the flag appeared out of the box. On the flag was written the word 'BANG'. Starky gave a startled laugh. He opened the box and found a black, toy imitation bomb from which the flag had burst like a jack-in-the-box. Inside was a typed message.

'This is a toy. The one you get next will be for real. Stop playing games. This is your last warning. Deliver the goods tonight or else your daughter and your girl friend will die.'

Starky re-read the note, and folded it neatly. He moved as if to return to his bungalow and hesitated. Perhaps he should forget Maddison. He looked grim. The pain at the nape of his neck had come back again.

But Maddison had not forgotten Starky. After a very early meeting with Weiderman and a check with the listening unit to confirm that there had been no telephone calls of importance, Maddison was anxious to meet Starky. He called for Mary at her home.

'I would like to take you to the plant,' he said seriously.

Mary realised that something was up. She hurriedly collected her belongings.

'See you tonight,' she called out to her mother.

'Yes, honey,' her mother replied. 'Your father will pick you up at the plant.'

They got into the car and drove away. Maddison switched on his radio set. It crackled. He left it on.

'Is this the big day?' Mary asked earnestly.

'Yes,' Maddison replied. 'It has to be today or never.'

'I hope it is never,' Mary said quietly.

'Why do you say that?' Maddison asked.

Mary shrugged. 'Oh! I don't know. Perhaps I don't like change,' she smiled. 'Perhaps I'm frightened someone is going to get hurt.'

'Harry Starky?' Maddison asked.

Mary blushed up.

'I wasn't thinking of him in particular,' she said hotly.

'Were you thinking of me?' Maddison asked, teasing her.

She looked away. 'You are impossible,' she said.

'Sorry that wasn't a fair question.'

He turned a corner and headed towards the highway.

'Mary,' he said seriously, 'I want you to promise me one thing.'

She looked at him.

'What, Gary?' she asked.

'No matter if anyone phones you or contacts you, I want you to promise me you will go nowhere near Harry Starky today or tonight. Keep well out of his way.'

'All right, Gary,' she said. 'I promise.'

'Starky has just left the estate and turned east on to the highway.' The message came over the radio and spurred Maddison into action. He glanced at his watch.

'We should meet him just before he arrives at the plant,' he said.

He increased his speed. He wanted to intercept Starky at the car park. Starky beat him by a short head. He was getting out of his car as Maddison pulled up alongside him. Starky looked tense. He came over to them.

'Anything?' Maddison asked pointedly.

Starky hesitated as if having a mental battle with himself. He looked slightly uncomfortable.

'Yeah,' he sighed. 'I got a message this morning along with a toy bomb.'

'A rather offbeat sense of humour,' Maddison said. 'Don't give me anything, just tell me.'

'This is my last chance,' Starky said. 'Either I deliver the goods today or my daughter,' he hesitated momentarily, 'or my friend,' he looked at Maddison who nodded his head understandingly, 'will be killed.'

'And how do you deliver?' Maddison asked.

Starky shrugged. 'Those details have yet to come,' he said. 'That's supposing I get what is needed,' he added ruefully.

'You'll get it,' Maddison said.

'What do I do?' Starky asked.

'Keep me posted. Call me immediately you are contacted.' He stressed the word 'immediately'. He turned to Mary.

'Is it O.K. if I drop you here?'

'Certainly.'

Mary got out of the car.

'Remember what I told you,' he called after her. 'Good luck, Harry.'

'Sure,' Starky said dryly, but he had a look about him that suggested that the whole of the F.B.I. and the Soviet spy system were watching him. Maddison watched them go through the gates of the Research Centre and then drove to the F.B.I.'s temporary headquarters at the ranch, out of town.

Weiderman greeted him by handing him a piece of paper.

'This is the answer to the questions you posed,' he said. 'It confirms your suspicions.'

Maddison read the information.

'Yes, he's our man,' he said slowly. 'He had to be.'

'He'll have an assistant,' Weiderman warned.

'Yes, that's the problem,' Maddison agreed.

'Funny case this,' Weiderman mused. 'It's almost like playing a game of wits. We could stop the game now and come out of it O.K.'

'But we won't,' Maddison added.

'No, that's the odd thing about it. We're going to see it through.'

'Can we really lose?' Maddison asked.

'I'm not sure. I have a feeling we are under-estimating them. They knew the sands would run out once they started the game. They took a calculated risk that they could keep us guessing right up to the end and they have to a certain extent. Can we say for sure who his accomplice is?'

'No,' Maddison agreed. 'I have my hunches.'

'They don't convict anyone,' Weiderman said seriously. 'Let us see it from his angle. He'll know we must be on to him. What's he going to do?'

'Make sure he has a get away. He's going to lose himself as quickly as possible. We've got to cover all exits. Rail, road, and air and that includes Jackson Field.'

'And his accomplice?' Maddison asked.

'Whoever it is is expendable,' Weiderman said. 'Our man is a Russian spy whose usefulness is finished. His accomplice is a dead duck.'

'Now all it needs is for Starky to get an opportunity to take the photographs and for us to lay our nets. It sounds too easy.'

'That's what worries me. It does sound too easy.'

Weiderman looked at the map in front of him.

'We can pick up Starky as soon as he leaves the plant. By tonight I'll have fifty men in the area all on our radio net. Wherever he goes after leaving the plant he'll be followed. The only blind spot is on the actual estate, but I'll fix that so we can keep the front of his bungalow covered from a field near the wood.'

'Supposing the camera doesn't leave the plant?'

Weiderman looked up at him. 'What do you think?' he asked.

'It'll come out,' Maddison agreed.

'Contact Starky as soon as he leaves the plant and see if he has the stuff.'

'By phone?'

'Yeah.'

'We'll put two rings around the town. One on all the roads leading out of town and another about ten miles out. Every car licence will be recorded. The Sheriff's men are going to help on the outer ring and Hugan's men will operate the inner one. Fortunately this place is not Chicago.'

'And the other escape routes?'

'We'll have the railroad station watched, the bus depot and Jackson Field. Incidentally, Hendrich has arranged for his plane to be fuelled tonight ready for an early start in the morning. Also Starky's.'

Maddison looked at Weiderman.

'He's done it before,' Weiderman added.

'A quick trip over into Canada and there's a lot of space to hide over there,' Maddison said.

'Could be.'

'What about the river?' Maddison asked. 'It's a way out of town.'

'Yeah,' Weiderman agreed. 'Good thinking. We'll have to watch that one.' He looked at the map. 'Could take a boat way past our road blocks, pick up a car and away.'

'What do we tell Hugan?' Maddison asked.

'You can put him partly in the picture. Use your discretion. He can make any arrests.'

'And our spy?'

'I'll leave him to you, but,' Weiderman added seriously, 'we've got to be prepared for anything. He's taken a big gamble already. I don't think he's finished yet. He may have an ace up his sleeve.'

'Where do you want me?' Maddison asked.

'To start off, I want you on the highway in case the drop is at Jackson Field. After that we'll play it over the radio.'

'Yes, chief.'

'Now, you had better get into town and brief the lieutenant. After that keep close to the plant and keep close to Harry Starky.'

'What about you?' Maddison asked.

'I have to meet the Senator's caravan,' Weiderman grumbled. 'Have you seen the morning papers?'

Maddison indicated that he had. 'Another victory for him in Minneapolis,' he said.

'Let's hope he doesn't add Medway

Springs to his list,' Weiderman warned. 'By the way, the Senator was asking about Hendrich.'

'Hendrich?' Maddison asked in surprise.

'Appears to be a generous donator to the Party,' Weiderman said.

'A generous sucker more likely,' Maddison added. 'Unless his ambitions are aimed at Washington.'

'Could be,' Weiderman sighed. 'Any rate, I'll take care of Senator Leebright. You look after Starky.'

'O.K. I wonder how he feels?'

Starky wasn't feeling too good. The pain at the back of his neck was playing him up again.

After dealing with his morning mail he went over to the research laboratory. He was admitted into the compound by one of the guards. Inside the front office Joe McIntyre greeted him cheerfully.

'Hi! Harry,' McIntyre called out. 'Everything O.K.?'

'Sure, Joe,' Starky replied. He entered the laboratory. Dr Kay was waiting for him. Ludvick and Benson were busy with some apparatus. Dr Cusack was in the small office with his reports. Starky and Kay got down to work. The morning passed slowly. The lunch time break was taken in the canteen. The laboratory was locked by McIntyre who remained in his office. The four scientists and Starky returned together.

In the afternoon, Starky and Kay became further engrossed in their work. There was a possibility that they would finish that afternoon. At about 4 p.m. Starky heard the phone ring in Cusack's office. He paid little heed to it. But a few seconds later an agitated Cusack appeared in the laboratory. He called the scientists together and held a brief conversation. Whatever it was, it didn't please Cusack. Cusack went away muttering under his breath.

'We are being summoned to meet Senator Leebright,' Kay explained to Starky.

'An important man,' Starky replied.

'I don't know why Logan doesn't bring him over here,' Ludvick complained.

'Probably wants to give him the V.I.P. treatment in the board room. Drinks and all that.'

Ludvick grunted.

'Sorry about this,' Kay said to Starky. 'We'll have to finish it off tomorrow.'

'I'll just complete this section dealing with the routine allowance,' Starky said.

'Perhaps you will be wanted, Mr Starky,' Cusack said. 'If so, I will phone you.'

'If they want this estimate finished this week they had better leave me alone.'

'Quite,' Cusack muttered. He closed his office door. The four scientists left the laboratory and Starky.

Starky continued with his work. In the outer office McIntyre sat at his desk. The two men could see each other through a glass screen. A few minutes later McIntyre became deeply engrossed in a telephone conversation. All Starky could see was McIntyre's back as he pored over some past reports. Starky gave a faint smile, and picked up his camera.

The time was five-fifteen precisely. At five-sixteen a very short, high frequency signal was picked up in the F.B.I.'s van parked close to the plant. Immediately the signal was received a message was sent around the network of F.B.I. agents. Emergency code RED was in operation. The code which meant there had been a breach of security. From that moment on it was no longer a game of cat and mouse.

THIRTEEN

Starky left the plant at 6 p.m. A watching eye reported his movement to Weiderman who was in a control unit at the junction of the two highways north of the town. A radio network was in operation manned by a small force of F.B.I. agents at various vantage points with their special radio sets. Hugan was on net at the precinct station east of town. His men were also spread out forming a ring around the town, as were the Sheriff's men about ten miles from the town centre. The police, except for a selected handful, were unaware what was taking place. Their orders were to keep out of sight, record all movement and be on call. Weiderman was well aware that the police radio messages could be picked up on the domestic car radio. He had thought of every possible contingency – or so he hoped.

Not only was Starky's departure and journey to the Riverside Estate closely followed, but so also were all the other suspects. Logan, Cusack and Ludvick all returned to their homes independently, as did Mrs Bradley. McIntyre and Kay remained at the plant. Benson returned to his apartment. He had a friend visiting him from Chicago and had arranged to meet him at the railroad station.

As soon as Starky was reported to have entered his bungalow, Maddison phoned him.

A rather subdued, hesitant Starky answered the call.

'Maddison here, have you been contacted?'

'Not yet,' Starky replied.

'You have the necessary information?'

There was a fractional pause which Maddison was quick to detect.

'Yeah,' Starky said, resignedly.

'Phone me immediately you are contacted.'

Maddison rang off. Vasey was standing alongside him in the trailer by the river. He smiled at Maddison.

'Do you think the guy's nervous?' he asked.

'Could be,' Maddison replied. 'It's a big night for him.' He glanced at his watch, it was six-thirty. He didn't expect much movement before dusk. This was going to be the worst part, he thought, the waiting – and the uncertainty.

But the time didn't drag, there was a lot of activity. The telephone wires became alive. Kay phoned Helen Logan from the plant and they arranged to meet at the Country Club later that evening. In the trailer Maddison, Vasey and the two other agents listened to the conversation. Kay was nervous, uncertain of himself. Helen Logan was the dominant partner in their affair. Their telephone conversation came to an abrupt end, when possibly Dr Logan had appeared in earshot. Diana Bradley telephoned the producer of her operatic society, Hank Warringer, and told him that she had managed to get hold of a prompter to fill the vacancy for their dress rehearsal that evening. Dr Ludvick and Dr Cusack held a brief conversation over some technical detail of Cusack's report. Cusack also phoned Logan and they arranged to go back to the plant to clear up a point which was giving Cusack some mental disturbance. Jayson Hendrich called Starky to confirm that Starky was going to pick him up at 8 a.m. to take him to Jackson Field the following morning.

Each time there was a call the agents became tense and alert, more so when Starky's number was involved.

At 7.45 p.m. precisely they got the first act

201

in their drama playlet.

'It's his!' one of the agents called out.

Maddison and Vasey picked up a headset.

Starky answered his call clearly.

'Starky,' he said.

'You have got it,' a voice said, not asking.

Starky didn't reply.

'Your instructions are in the blue folder in your briefcase,' the voice continued. 'Contact no one or the deal is off, do you understand?'

'Yeah,' Starky said. There was a trace of nervousness in his voice.

'You had better,' the voice warned. 'I will know if you do and that means curtains for you know who.'

The line went dead.

'Still think you have heard the voice before?' Vasey asked.

'It's a disguised voice, probably muffled, but we must have heard it.'

'Do you think he will phone you the details?' Vasey asked.

'No,' Maddison replied. The threat and change of plans in giving Starky his instructions were not unexpected.

'Hold it,' someone called out. 'He's phoning.'

They heard the phone ringing and then

Mrs Pringle, Maddison's landlady's voice came over loud and clear. It must be Starky, Maddison thought.

'Hullo,' she said. 'Double two three four seven.'

'I would like to speak to Mr Maddison,' Starky said.

'One moment,' Mrs Pringle said calmly. 'I'll fetch him.'

Maddison turned to tell the engineer to plug him in as he had arranged with Mrs Pringle. Suddenly the line went dead.

'What is it?' Maddison asked hurriedly.

'His line has been cut,' the agent replied. 'It's dead!'

'Very neat,' Vasey remarked.

'Yeah,' Maddison agreed. 'That's one way of solving the problem.'

'What now?' the agent at the set asked Maddison.

'Monitor the rest of the calls,' Maddison said. 'We will take up our positions. Tell Weiderman that we are going over to the radio.'

Maddison and Vasey returned to their car and took up their position on the East-West highway.

'Car mobile,' a voice said over the radio.

It was dusk. Very soon it would be dark,

Maddison thought, and everything would take on a different intensity.

The two agents listened closely.

'It's Logan and Cusack,' the radio reported. 'Leaving the estate now in a Buick, licence number…'

The message was no sooner noted than another came behind it.

'Benson has arrived at the railroad station,' came a report.

'How did he get through the net?' Weiderman asked authoritatively.

'Arrived by cab,' came a reply.

'Don't lose him,' Weiderman ordered. 'Keep him under surveillance.'

'Here comes Madam Butterfly,' a voice reported. 'She's early tonight.'

Vasey lit a cigarette. Maddison sat quietly looking out of his window.

'What's her licence number?' a voice demanded. It was Weiderman.

He got the information immediately.

'Thank you,' Weiderman said.

'That's Logan and Cusack,' Vasey said. He picked up the microphone. 'Logan turning off the highway to town,' he reported.

'Starky mobile!'

Maddison sat upright. He saw Mrs Bradley drive past. In the darkness he couldn't make out what costume she was wearing. She seemed in a hurry.

'Bradley turned off to town,' Vasey reported.

'Kay left the plant,' a voice reported, 'going west.' To the Country Club, Maddison thought.

'Here comes Starky,' he said. He watched him go by and saw his light-coloured suit and trilby. He sat hunched up over the steering wheel.

'Starky turning into town,' Vasey reported.

'Logan going to the plant,' a voice reported. Maddison recognised the voice. It was Hugan.

Maddison watched Starky's car disappear in the distance and started the engine.

'Vasey, mobile,' Vasey reported. 'Following Starky.' Maddison moved into the correct lane.

'The Bradley woman is turning into West Street,' Hugan reported.

Going to the High School, Maddison thought. He took the turning into town. Starky should be approaching Hugan now. He breathed heavily. Unconsciously he found himself gripping the wheel.

'Starky turning into Main Street,' Hugan said. 'I'm following.'

'Bradley dame crossed over West and North Street,' a voice reported.

She hadn't stopped at the High School, Maddison thought. He wondered why. It irritated him because it was not what he had expected.

He was not the only one who felt an inner warning. So did Lieutenant Hugan. Sitting in a civilian car alongside Sergeant Shean, he instinctively sensed that something was wrong. He said nothing to the sergeant who had his eye fixed firmly on Starky's car as it moved along Main Street to the centre of the town. Hugan wondered what Mrs Bradley was up to. He heard a report come over the radio about Logan's movements. It was followed by another reporting that Helen Logan had left the estate.

'He's turning south,' Sergeant Shean said.

'The railroad station,' Hugan growled. He turned to one of the detectives in the rear. 'Report it,' he told them.

The detective passed the message.

'Get closer,' Hugan ordered. The sergeant increased his speed.

'The Chicago train is due to leave about now,' the sergeant warned. 'It'll be very busy.'

'Yeah, I know,' Hugan replied. 'There's

also the train due out for St Paul.' But his mind was still thinking about Mrs Bradley. There had been no further message about her movements and it troubled him.

They passed the Police Headquarters and Metropol Hotel. A cab cut in on them blocking their view. The sergeant swore. Another message came over the air, but not about the Bradley woman.

'He's turning,' the sergeant said.

'Report it,' Hugan snapped.

Starky was held up at the turning into the forecourt of the railroad station. There was a lot of activity. A hell of a lot, Hugan thought. Taxi cabs were pouring in and out of the area.

Sergeant Shean pulled up two cars behind Starky.

'What do we do inside?' he asked. 'Follow him?' Hugan didn't reply. He was watching Starky. He had stalled his car. Suddenly it shot forward. Hugan saw Starky hunched across the wheel as if he was gripping it nervously with two hands.

'Where is the Bradley dame?' someone asked anxiously over the radio. It was Maddison.

'Last seen heading west at the junction of West and North,' came the reply.

So Maddison was anxious as well, Hugan thought.

'Get in behind Starky,' he ordered.

The sergeant swung out and overtook the two cars. A cab driver coming the other way blasted his horn at them. One of the car drivers yelled abuse. The sergeant swung into the station area.

Starky had turned into the park in front of the entrance. He was making for the far end of the park which bordered an open area used as a lumber yard.

'Pull up here,' Hugan ordered, pointing to the sidewalk. They were facing the station. Starky was moving way over to their right.

'The F.B.I. got their man here?' Sergeant Shean asked.

'Yeah,' Hugan replied thoughtfully. He was watching Starky. He had misjudged his turn into a parking lot and was trying to sort himself out, but he appeared as if he was trying to get as close as possible to the lumber yard.

'He's having a busy time,' the sergeant said.

'Yeah,' Hugan agreed thoughtfully. That does it, he thought to himself. He gritted his teeth. It was a hunch, but he knew his hunches. He turned to a detective in the rear seat with the radio set.

'Tell them I'm going in to arrest Starky,' he ordered.

The sergeant looked at him sharply.

'Starky?' he asked.

'Yeah,' Hugan growled. 'Don't let that guy get away,' he added. 'Come on.'

Hugan got out of his car. The sergeant followed.

'Quickly before he disappears into the lumber yard,' Hugan shouted.

They brushed past a group of people and ran along the parking lot. They saw Starky walking away from his car, a briefcase in his hand. He must have sensed the danger. He half turned, saw Hugan running towards him and started to run for it. He headed for the darkness of the lumber yard.

The sergeant swore. Hugan cut through the cars.

'He's making for the yard,' Hugan shouted. They were going to lose him, he thought desperately. Suddenly a figure stepped out from the shadows and bumped heavily into Starky. Starky went sprawling to the ground. Breathlessly, Hugan and Sergeant Shean ran up to the floored figure.

'Thanks,' Hugan said. Sergeant Shean was bending over the figure on the ground.

'O.K. Lieutenant,' the man said, who had

assisted them.

Sergeant Shean picked up the floored figure and his mouth fell open in surprise. It was not Harry Starky! It was Diana Bradley! Her hair had fallen away from the band which had kept it tight under her trilby. It hung over her face. Her necktie was half way round her neck.

The sergeant recovered from his surprise and gripped her arm firmly.

'Where's Starky?' Hugan snapped.

'I don't know what you are talking about,' Diana Bradley said scornfully.

'You know all right,' Hugan fumed. 'Where is he?'

Diana Bradley laughed.

'Go to hell, Lieutenant,' she said.

A couple of cars screamed into the forecourt. In one of them was Maddison. A small crowd gathered around. They were being kept back by two plain clothes agents.

'Take her to the car,' Hugan snapped.

'What for?' Diana Bradley asked scornfully. 'What have I done wrong?'

'You're under arrest,' Hugan said.

'On what charge?'

'Accessory to first degree murder,' Hugan snarled.

'Murder!' Diana Bradley exclaimed. 'You'll

never prove it.'

'I've heard that before,' Hugan snapped. 'Take her, sergeant.' Sergeant Shean pushed her through the crowd. He was joined by a uniformed patrolman. Hugan saw Maddison. He went over to him.

'It's the Bradley dame,' he said.

Maddison looked at him. 'My God,' he said. 'Then...' He didn't finish the sentence. He turned, got in the seat that Vasey had vacated, and picked up the radio microphone.

'Maddison here,' he said instantly. 'Hugan has arrested Diana Bradley. She was impersonating Starky. There has been a switch. Locate Bradley's car immediately.'

'O.K.' Weiderman came back to him. 'This is priority,' he added. 'Get Hugan to put out a general call.'

Maddison turned to Hugan.

'I got it,' Hugan said. 'There's a patrol car in the forecourt.'

'Use code,' Maddison warned.

Hugan grunted and left Maddison in the car.

'She was seen going west at the junction of North and West,' a voice reported, 'at eight-thirty.'

'What about that junction with the highway?' Weiderman asked over the air.

'No sign of her here, Chief,' a voice reported.

'He must still be in the box,' Weiderman said, 'or switched cars.'

Switched cars! Maddison looked at his map. How could he have switched cars? They had been so close to him the last three days that they knew his every movement. If he had switched cars then there was another accomplice.

'Where are the rest?' he asked over the radio.

'All accounted for,' Weiderman replied. 'McIntyre and Kay are at the Club. Logan and Cusack are at the plant. Ludvick is at his bungalow with his wife.'

'Benson?'

'At the station. He is being detained there for the time being.'

'Hendrich?' Maddison asked anxiously.

'At the Club,' Weiderman replied.

'What about the wives?'

'Negative,' came the reply. 'All accounted for.' There was a pause. 'Except Mary Lewis. You fixed her?'

'Yeah,' Maddison replied. 'She's at home.'

'You better check it out,' Weiderman said. 'I'll have the area combed.'

Mary? Maddison felt his stomach turn

over. He had told her to keep well out of Starky's way. She had promised, but had she kept to it? He got out of the car. Vasey looked at him. 'There's a telephone in the foyer,' he said. 'Here are some nickels.'

Maddison grabbed the money. Mary just had to be at her home, he thought. He ran into the foyer, found an empty booth and dialled the number.

It was Mary's father who answered the call.

'Gary here,' Maddison said anxiously. 'I would like to speak to Mary.'

'Oh! Mary has gone out, Gary,' Mr Lewis said.

'Out!' Maddison exclaimed. 'Where?'

'She arranged to meet Mrs Bradley from the plant,' Mr Lewis explained. Maddison's heart sank. 'She agreed to help her with the rehearsals. Mary has done...'

Mr Lewis went on to explain how Mary had often acted as prompter for the musical society. Maddison heard the explanation, but his brain was way ahead on another track. She had gone to meet Mrs Bradley thinking she was safe and out of the way. Maddison inwardly groaned. It couldn't have been worse.

'Where did Mary arrange to meet her?'

Maddison asked.

'At the library on the corner of Vincent Street.'

'Near the North-South highway?'

'Yeah.'

'What time?'

'Eight-thirty. Why all the questions, Gary? Is everything O.K.?'

'It will be,' Maddison said evasively. 'Which car was she driving?'

'My saloon.'

'What make is it?' Maddison asked impatiently. 'And licence number?'

'It's a grey Chevrolet saloon. Licence number SJC 3478.'

'Radio?'

'Yeah. Gary, is Mary in danger?'

'I don't know,' Maddison lied. 'Just stay where you are and I'll be in touch.'

He replaced the receiver before Mr Lewis had time to ask any further questions. Blast! He thought. Blast! Blast!

He stormed out of the booth and rushed back to where Hugan and a group of F.B.I. agents were standing.

'Mary has gone to meet Mrs Bradley,' Maddison explained hurriedly to Hugan. 'Arranged to meet her at the library at eight-thirty.'

Hugan realised the implication. He saw the concern on Maddison's face.

'Switched cars?' Hugan asked.

'Yeah.'

Maddison grabbed the microphone and reported to Weiderman.

'Get Hugan to put out a general call to all cars in code,' Weiderman ordered. 'I'll contact the road blocks and report back.'

'O.K.'

Maddison turned to Hugan. 'He wants a general call to all cars, in code. We have to find either Bradley's car or Mary's. She is using her father's.' He gave Hugan a description of the car and its licence number.

'O.K.,' Hugan said. He went over to one of the police cars and sent out the message. When he returned, Maddison was standing with clenched fists. He looked grim.

'How long have we got?' Hugan asked.

Maddison looked at his watch. It was eight-fifty. 'Another twenty-six minutes,' he said anxiously.

There was a garbled message over the car radio. Vasey called to Maddison. Maddison hurriedly picked up the microphone.

'Maddison.'

'They passed through the first road block heading west about twenty minutes ago in

Lewis's car,' Weiderman reported.

'Heading west?' Maddison asked with surprise.

'Yeah, towards Railton.'

'And Pine Creek!' Maddison added thoughtfully.

'We've got another road block west of Railton,' Weiderman explained. 'We can stop them there if we have to.'

'Have to? What do you mean?' Maddison asked.

'He's desperate,' Weiderman explained. 'The girl is driving. He'll have her covered.'

Hugan overheard the conversation. Pine Creek! Railton! That's where the second murder had taken place. At Hendrich's lodge. Coincidence? he wondered. Why was Starky going west? The obvious place had been Jackson Field. Starky was a flier. Something clicked into place inside his brain. Flier! Hell! Jake Cullen!

'Gary!' he called out sharply. Maddison looked up at him, questioningly. 'There's a plane on the lake at Pine Creek,' Hugan explained. 'Came in one night last week. It's about two miles south west of the town. Hidden away.'

Maddison picked up the microphone and told Weiderman.

'He should be arriving in Pine Creek in about ten minutes,' Maddison added.

'Hold it!' Hugan called out.

'Wait,' Maddison said into the microphone.

'We have to think of Mary,' Hugan said, between his clenched teeth. 'If they pass through Pine Creek then you have to stop them at the road block. You have no alternative. If he's using that plane on the lake you'll never get anyone to them in time. They'll make enough noise to warn Starky a mile away, and they don't know the tracks.'

'So?' Maddison asked. 'What do you suggest?'

'I know somebody who will help,' Hugan said and held Maddison firmly in his eyes. 'Let's give it a try.'

'O.K. John,' Maddison said quietly. 'Go ahead.'

FOURTEEN

Mary Lewis gripped the steering wheel of her car and stared straight ahead of her at the on-coming, dark highway. She had got over the initial shock of being confronted by Harry Starky masquerading as Mrs Bradley in her theatrical costume and the realisation that Starky was the man the F.B.I. were after. The man responsible for two murders and the spy who had dangled the bait to the F.B.I. It was this realisation, more than the ridiculous get-up, that had shaken her composure. Harry Starky had used her just as he had used everyone else to get the information he wanted. It hurt her pride. Not that she had been in love with Harry Starky, but she had trusted him. She had considered him a close friend. This broken trust hurt her deeply. She saw some headlamps ahead at a crossroad. It looked like a road block. It made her pulse quicken. Starky also saw them and fingered his revolver.

'Don't stop,' he said pointedly, 'and don't try to signal them. I would hate to have to use this.' He moved the briefcase on his lap to show the revolver.

Mary didn't reply. She wondered where Gary was, and the rest of his men. Gary had suspected Starky for a long time, she thought. She knew that now. Some of his remarks began to make sense. She wondered what he would think when he found out that she was now in Starky's company. The very thing that he had tried to avoid. She mentally sighed. She wasn't to know that Mrs Bradley and Starky were in league – no one was.

Starky watched the parked vehicles come closer. He had expected them. This would be the road block around the town, he thought. Once past them and he was flying. And there was no reason why they should stop them. They wouldn't be looking for Mary's father's car. His face broke into a satisfied smile. At the very worst they would be looking for Diana Bradley's car. At the best they would be following a false trail, and why should they even be doing that? he wondered. There had been no sign of anyone watching them. It had all gone according to plan. Diana Bradley, dressed as Harry Starky, would have got into the lumber yard and then aboard the 8.55 p.m. train for Chicago. They had rehearsed it all before. They even had a secret hideaway in the yard with a change of disguise ready. If Diana Bradley had got into the lumber yard, then she was home and dry. They had played it very carefully. And even if that had gone wrong, so what? She was expendable. She had outlived her usefulness. So long as he got away, over the border into Canada, nothing else mattered, but he was glad he wasn't going to be around to tell her. He wondered how long she would lie low in New York before realising that she had been ditched. He grunted audibly and twisted his mouth as he thought of all their meetings – meetings making plans, giving promises – and sex. Oh, yes, Starky thought, above all else, sex. Diana Bradley craved for it like the frustrated nymphomaniac that she was. That had been her downfall and Starky's ammunition. Once the Communists had established her frustration she had been like putty in their hands. It had been very considerate of Logan to allocate them the two bungalows detached from the others. Starky recalled the first encounter he had with her. He had gone to wish her a Happy Christmas. It had been their first Christmas at the plant – in fact Starky had only been at the plant a couple of weeks. He had found her dressed in a flimsy, silk dressing gown and slightly the worse for drink. That had been the beginning of their affair. From then on, she would do anything for him, anything! But there had been no need for her to strip Laura Nolan's body and put it in that grotesque pose, he thought. No need at all. That had been Diana Bradley's twisted mind again. It was not as it had been planned. If he had left the body as Diana Bradley had left it, the police would have known the type of person they were looking for.

They came to the crossroads. Starky counted six cars, three either side of the highway. He could see a group of uniformed cops, but there was no move to stop them.

'So long, suckers,' he muttered more to himself than to Mary. He took off his wig, it was making him perspire.

'How far are we going?' Mary asked nervously.

'Pine Creek,' Starky replied confidently. 'I have a plane on the lake.'

'What about me?'

'You are my passport against anything going wrong,' Starky said evenly. 'You come with me.' He needed her, even when they were airborne, against any possible reprisals.

'All the way?' Mary asked hesitantly.

'All the way,' Starky agreed, 'until I get to where I want to be.' He held the revolver up so that she could see it from the corner of her eye.

'So long as you do as I say,' he added, 'no harm will come to you. You will be safe and alive when it is all over, but if you don't...' He shrugged. 'I will be forced to use this. I don't want to. Understand?'

Mary nodded her head.

'O.K.,' he said. 'Now put your foot down.'

Mary pressed the accelerator pedal and the car responded. It wouldn't take them long to get to Pine Creek, she thought. No one could stop them, now.

Starky undid his dress and struggled out of it. He unrolled his trousers which he had been wearing under the dress and fastened his collar.

He felt much better. There was no pain any longer at the back of his neck. The doctor at the plant had been correct in thinking it was a tension pain, he thought. Starky had been tense all right. He had been tense ever since 2nd June, but not any more. In fact, he felt elated. In a few minutes he would be airborne and a short flight to his rendezvous over the border. After that? Well, he was finished now with the States. He would be sent home, where he would get an inside job. Home! The thought excited him. There were people he longed to see. His family, his friends. He had served the Party well. He had earned his rest. He had murdered and lied for them. Surely they would reward him now, and all he wanted was to belong again.

'Did you have to kill Laura Nolan?' Mary asked.

Her remark interrupted Starky's thoughts of home and irritated him.

'Yes,' he said gruffly. 'We had to get rid of her. She refused to go through with our plans and wanted out.'

'And the man at Hendrich's lodge?'

'He tried to do a double deal,' Starky grunted. 'He got greedy.'

'Why did you need him in the first place?' Mary asked.

'He was part of the scenery,' Starky replied patiently. 'I give a colourful story of my night out which was almost a hundred per cent true, but none of it could be sub-stantiated and everything looked as if I was either lying or being framed. I became the central figure in Laura Nolan's murder. I attracted all the attention. So much so that I could make the F.B.I. play right into my hands. No one knew if I was telling the truth or not. I've used them all – the fools.'

'Why should you want all the attention?' Mary asked. 'Couldn't you just take what you wanted?'

'No more questions,' Starky snapped. 'It will soon be time for action.'

They came to the switchback which preceded the drop into Pine Creek.

'There is a track leading into the wood at the top of the hill,' Starky said. 'Take it.'

Mary saw the opening and turned off the highway.

'Dip your headlamps,' Starky ordered.

Mary did as he ordered. She was beginning to feel anxious. They were following a rough, dirt track, which made the car bounce about. Ahead of them was a dark mass of trees which surrounded the lake. It was like a jungle. Few people ever used that side of the lake. It was a protected area. No one would stop them now, she thought. She could feel panic grip her and she pulled herself together abruptly. She had to keep a grip of herself. To think constructively, not destructively. Somehow she had to escape from him. It shouldn't be difficult. It was dark. If she could get out of his immediate vicinity she could get lost in the wood. But the moment had to be right.

Almost as if Starky was reading her thoughts, he moved the revolver closer to her body. He said nothing, but the gesture warned her that he was watching for any surprise move. She contemplated crashing the car, swinging it off the track, but they weren't travelling fast enough for it to make any great impact. She drove on slowly, negotiating the uneven, winding surface. Occasionally they would disturb some wild fowl which would screech its way into the sky. The track seemed never ending and the tension in the car was building up. Once she asked him how far they were going along the track, but he abruptly ordered her to be quiet. She could sense that he was tense, like herself. When eventually he ordered her to stop, the relief was enormous.

'Lights out,' Starky said, and opened his car door.

Mary switched out the lights and the darkness enveloped them. She opened her car door.

'This side,' Starky ordered. 'Follow me.'

He backed out of the car, one hand pulling Mary after him, the other holding the revolver and his briefcase. They stood for a while until Starky became accustomed to the dim light of a quarter moon, then he pushed her along a narrow path through the woods. They stumbled forward, brushing against projecting foliage which caught their clothes.

They came to a clearing and across the lake they could see the lights of Railton. Starky got his bearings and pushed Mary forward again. Tensely, silently, they worked their way around the lake for about ten minutes.

They came to a small landing bay. Starky grunted, 'This is it.' He pulled her towards some bushes. She tried to resist.

'Don't make me get rough,' Starky snapped. 'Under that shrubbery you'll find a rubber dinghy. Get it out.'

He stood back, behind her. She half expected him to hit her. She pulled the bushes aside and felt the boat.

'Pull it out,' Starky ordered.

She dragged it out of the bushes and pulled it towards the water's edge. Starky pushed it into the lake.

'Get in,' he ordered.

Mary hesitated.

'Hold it!' a strange voice suddenly called out. It made them both start. Starky grabbed Mary and swung around.

'Not so fast, Mister,' the voice called out again from the darkness. It was an unusual, drawling voice, with a local country accent.

'I've got a bead on you,' the voice said again from a different direction.

Starky swung Mary around again to face the direction of the voice.

'Let the lady go,' the voice said again, 'or I'll wing you.'

Starky fired twice into the darkness from where the voice had come.

Crack! Thud! A bullet smacked into the tree above their heads.

'You shouldn't have done that, Mister,' the voice drawled.

Again Starky fired.

Crack! A bullet smacked into the ground near Starky's feet. It made him jump. His hand let go of Mary.

'Run for it, lady!' the voice called out and another bullet smacked into the ground near Starky. Starky grabbed at Mary, but she broke free and ran wildly into the bushes. Two more rifle shots rang out. Mary ran up the bank, crashing through the trees. Frantically she ran for her life. Suddenly an arm pulled her to the ground.

'You're O.K. Missy,' a man said. 'Just stay where you are.'

Mary fell to the ground and stifled a sob.

'The critter's in the dinghy now,' the man said. 'You are all right. You can stand up.'

A hand lifted Mary on to her feet.

'Who are you?' she gasped, looking into a bearded face.

'Name is Jake Cullen,' the man said, 'but folks round here call me Beaver.'

She saw a tall, slim figure with a long poker face surrounded by an untidy beard. He was wearing dark, rough, hunting clothes.

'Who told you about him?' Mary asked hesitantly.

'Lieutenant Hugan,' Beaver replied. 'He phoned me at the Tavern.'

'Where is he going?' Mary asked, meaning Starky.

'Come with me, Missy,' Beaver said.

He led her down to the water's edge.

'That critter's got a plane hidden in the bushes off the point,' he explained. 'You can only get to it by boat. The ground is too marshy.' He brought out his pipe from his jacket pocket. 'Came across it accidentally a week ago.' He lit his pipe. 'I wondered where he had put it,' he added. 'It landed here early one morning. Fair gave me a shock. Messed up some of my nets.'

Mary listened to Beaver's casual chatter.

He was so relaxed, so unconcerned. She gave a nervous laugh.

'Take it easy, Missy,' Beaver said encouragingly. 'Everything's all right now. The lieutenant will soon be in Pine Creek with your friends.'

'But he is getting away!' Mary exclaimed pointing to the lake.

'Not so fast,' Beaver warned. 'He'll not get far.'

'You've emptied the tank?' Mary asked anxiously.

'Not me,' Beaver replied. 'I wouldn't know where to look.'

They heard an engine leap into life. Starky was set to make his flight. Beaver pulled out a luminous watch from his jacket pocket. The plane moved forward. The pitch of its engine got higher. Suddenly they saw a faint orange glow on the lake. It seemed to grow in size until suddenly a sheet of flame stabbed the darkness. Mary looked aghast as she saw the flames become brighter. There was a loud explosion as the fuel ignited. The flames vanished, leaving the darkness and debris.

'That's it,' Beaver said sadly.

'But what happened?' Mary stammered.

'There was some self destroying device set

to go off at sixteen minutes past nine,' Beaver explained, 'and it did. It sure is amazing what electrical gadgets they can make these days. I remember reading...'

Mary heard Beaver's voice trail away. She felt her legs go weak. An arm caught her before she fainted.

Maddison saw Mary safely into the police car.

'You are sure you are O.K.?' he asked through the open window.

Mary smiled encouragingly

'Sure, Gary. I'll be all right.'

'I'll see you later. It won't take long.'

He stood back and gave the uniformed policeman the O.K. The police car moved away and Maddison walked back to the Tavern which had become the F.B.I.'s temporary headquarters, just as Pine Creek had become the assembly area for an army of police cars. It only needed the Senator's caravan to arrive to complete the gathering.

In an upstairs room Maddison joined Hugan and Sergeant Shean and a number of F.B.I. agents who had been ordered to remain for Weiderman's de-briefing conference. Weiderman was deep in conversation with an agent who had brought him some up-to-date information.

One of the company produced a bottle and a number of glasses and the men silently helped themselves. There was a tense expectancy about the atmosphere which was suddenly pierced by a wailing police siren that heralded the arrival of Senator Leebright.

Weiderman and Maddison exchanged quick glances. They heard car doors being opened and slammed.

'You'd think it was the President himself,' Hugan hissed.

'That's his ambition,' someone replied.

A few seconds later the room door burst open and Senator Leebright stormed into their midst with his usual dynamic electrifying aplomb. With him was his number one man, Julius Stein.

Leebright came into the centre of the room and stood serious faced, slightly bent, with his jacket resting over his shoulders. The dark haired, bespectacled Stein stood behind him, as usual. He was the same height as the Senator, but looked more academic and meaner. There was nothing casual about his dress. It was neat and correct.

The Senator surveyed the room and was satisfied that he had made the right type of impression.

'Evening, Sam,' he said to Weiderman.

'Good evening, Senator,' Weiderman replied, and addressed the assembled company. 'You all know Senator Leebright,' he said, 'and his assistant, Mr Stein.' He turned to the Senator. 'These are all my men except Lieutenant Hugan and Sergeant Shean of Homicide.' He indicated the two men concerned. The Senator looked at them.

'You've done a good job, Lieutenant, and your men,' he said.

Hugan accepted the praise without comment.

'You have all done a good job,' the Senator added. 'It's men like you that keep the country clean.'

'We aren't quite finished, Senator,' Weiderman said quietly.

'So you told me on the phone,' the Senator replied. 'Well, you go ahead, Sam. Don't worry about Julius and me. We consider ourselves privileged to be allowed to be witnesses at your conference.'

'Thank you,' Weiderman said. He turned to his agents. 'I don't want to keep you longer than necessary,' he said. 'You have all done well and are to be congratulated.' He looked at Lieutenant Hugan. 'Thanks for your help, Lieutenant,' he said. 'You satisfied you got your murderer?'

'Yeah, we got our murderer,' Hugan agreed.

'Every case we come across,' Weiderman said, 'has its own peculiarities. Each one is different. We learn from them all, that's why I want to go back through this case.' From the corner of his eye he saw the Senator put a cigar in his mouth and signal to Stein to light it. 'At the beginning,' Weiderman continued, 'we were puzzled as to how the Russians got to know so much about the project. Once they were informed their interest was natural. Cusack's work hasn't been given any publicity, but he has managed a breakthrough which will be of vital importance. There weren't many people aware of this so the Russians must have got it from somebody directly concerned with the research. This was problem number one. Then Laura Nolan's murder presented further problems. Why had she been murdered and why implicate Starky? Laura Nolan became a Communist when she teamed up with Karl Lacey in Chicago. It is obvious that she came to the plant to work for the Communists. She followed the usual pattern of talent spotting, looking for a possible source of obtaining the necessary information, but then she found out that the Russians weren't particularly bothered. What they wanted was for Laura Nolan to fly to South America with Lacey, and take the rap for the leak. She was to be the scapegoat. Laura Nolan refused to do this and consequently she had to be disposed of. So she was murdered by Harry Starky. Correct. Lieutenant?'

'Yeah. Starky admitted to Mary Lewis that he did it,' Hugan said. 'We had our suspicions of him from the start, but couldn't figure out the timing. When we found the Bradley dame was in league with him it fitted into place.'

Weiderman gave him the O.K. to explain his point further. The agents listened intently to the lieutenant's explanation.

'Starky left his bungalow at seven-thirty,' he explained. 'Drove to the parking lot at the rear of the Central Garage. He then walked the three blocks to where Mrs Bradley's car was parked on a spare lot opposite the High School, next to the janitor's house. Starky took her car and drove to his meeting with Laura Nolan. It was now turning dark. After he strangled her, he put her body in the boot of Bradley's car, returned the car to where he had picked it up. The Bradley dame later dumped the body in his bungalow, whilst Starky was at Luigi's saloon.'

'And the Irish cabbie?' Weiderman asked.

'A well-known mobster from Chicago,' Hugan explained. 'Sell his soul for money. Mrs Bradley hired him, but he got greedy and put the squeeze on Starky. He had made a couple of calls from the roadhouse here in Pine Creek to a woman. That would have been to Mrs Bradley. He tried to squeeze more money out of her. She refused. He tried Starky, which was his downfall. Starky realised that the man had become a liability and came out during the night and shot him with Hendrich's gun.'

'Fortunately for Starky,' Weiderman said, 'he had had no contact with the cabbie, so when he tried to put the squeeze on Starky, Starky was able to put it to his advantage. He got Maddison to listen to the conversation. Starky was a smart operator.'

There was a general murmur of approval.

'That clears up the two murders,' Weiderman added, 'but it doesn't explain why Starky had the finger pointed at him.' Weiderman looked at Maddison and indicated that he could take over.

'Starky told Mary Lewis that he wanted to be centre of attraction,' Maddison explained. 'He wanted to be the central figure and yet not get himself arrested. It was important not to get himself arrested, and he succeeded. Although the lieutenant suspected Starky, he couldn't pin him down.'

There were also pressures brought to bear, Hugan thought, and glowered at the Senator, whose eyes were fixed on Maddison and didn't feel the lieutenant's resentment.

'Starky had to make it look as if he was being framed,' Maddison continued, 'so that when we came on the scene we would think he was being pushed to get the information of Cusack's research. It was a clever scheme. They knew we would go through with it because we reckoned we could outsmart them at the end. They thought the same. It didn't matter if we thought the threat to Starky was a bluff or not. They wanted us to play ball, and we did. If the police were put in the picture the deal was off. This was so that they could contain the play. They knew we would agree. It meant we couldn't get too close to our spy. They thought it also meant that a tap on Starky's phone or a close watch on him was out of the question. Starky had it all his own way. He arranged for the threat to his ex-wife and daughter to come when Mary Lewis was with him because he was aware of her uncle's association with the

Bureau. The phone calls were all pre-arranged tapes played by Diana Bradley. Starky acted his part even when there was no one around, just in case his phone was being tapped. He couldn't afford to take any risks. Diana Bradley gave him the camera and other messages which she got sent to her along with her pornographic literature from their New York contact. It was all neatly planned. We fell in line with the scheme. Starky was given a green pass. He was allowed into the laboratory and pushed into a situation where he could possibly have access to the information. By this time we were ourselves convinced that Starky was our man. He was probably aware of this. We didn't know who his accomplice was and that was his ace card. At the final play off, he and Diana Bradley made the switch and Starky nearly got away with it. That's how we see it.'

'Who actually was Starky?' one of the group asked.

'A very good actor for one thing,' Maddison said, 'and a professional at his job. As for who he really was – well, there is a period of five to six months just before Starky returned to the States when he toured the Continent. Probably during this period the real Harry Starky was eliminated and someone very like Starky assumed his identity. The Communists would have all the necessary information from Starky's wife who was then living in Poland. This we can only guess at, at this stage, but the picture we built up of Starky from former employers doesn't quite fit with the Starky we know. The original Harry Starky was a drifter, spendthrift, good timer, who played the horses. This is not the Starky we know.'

There was a general murmur of agreement. The Senator took the break in the debriefing to say his five cents worth.

'You and your boys have done a good job, Sam,' he said, nodding his head like a public benefactor. 'The country should get to know more about your work.' He turned to his assistant. 'Remind me, Julius,' he said, 'to make reference to these guys in my next big public address.'

'Yes, Senator,' Julius Stein said in a cold, bored manner which created a general feeling of antagonism towards him from the rest of the room. They had a strong desire to see him cut down to size.

'What gives now, Sam?' the Senator asked.

'We're not quite through,' Weiderman explained.

'More to come?' the Senator asked. 'This is better than a double feature,' he joked.

Weiderman again looked at Maddison.

'What the Communists attempted,' Maddison said, 'was a very involved way of getting information. So involved as to make us take a closer look at their reasons.'

Lieutenant Hugan watched the young agent with growing admiration.

'Laura Nolan was a small cog in the machine,' Maddison went on, 'and expendable. She knew very little of what was going on. She hadn't got access to classified information even though she was a secretary to the four scientists. If the Russians intended to use her it could only mean that she was going to get the information from someone, or someone else was going to give it to them separately. Similarly with the way Starky was supposedly being pushed. Someone else was a traitor. Someone who could give Starky or the Russians direct, the necessary information. If we accept that premise the field at Medway Springs is narrowed down to only six possible suspects. The four scientists, Logan and McIntyre. A good case could quite easily be built up against any one of them for making them suspect number one and for a variety of reasons. Cusack is anti-fascist, so is Benson. They resented Ludvick's role in the research. Ludvick has relations in East Germany. McIntyre could have been a mercenary. Logan could have been out for revenge.'

'Revenge?' the Senator asked.

'Yes, it was possible,' Maddison said calmly. 'He doesn't particularly like you, Senator, or the fact that you had an affair with his wife.'

'Now you look here, sonny,' the Senator fumed.

'It's only a theory, Senator,' Weiderman intervened sharply. 'We had to consider all possibilities.'

'I don't like it Sam. I'm warning you. Tell your boy to watch his remarks.'

'It was a possible theory,' Maddison continued, unperturbed. Hugan stifled a smile. The Senator glowered. 'Logan could have been got at when he was in Washington. The others could also have been got at. Any one of them might have been prepared to sell the secrets, or give them away for a multitude of reasons, but there was one weakness to this.' The room became very quiet. 'If any of those men could get access to the information then why was it necessary for Starky to go to the lengths he did? All that was needed was for one of the six to get a copy of the report and pass it over to the Russians, or Starky, at some later date. The deadline of today was not vital. We know that the Russians are greedy for the information, even desperate, but not to the extent of losing two good agents, like Starky and Bradley. Unless they were protecting a bigger fish.

Maddison caught the electric atmosphere in the room. He got an encouraging look from Hugan.

'The information had to appear to have been given to the Russians,' he continued, 'whilst it was still the responsibility of Logan, McIntyre and the unit at Medway Springs, because after that it became the direct responsibility of you, Senator Leebright.' Maddison looked directly at the Senator.

'Meaning just what?' the Senator fumed.

'Meaning, Senator,' Maddison said, holding the Senator firmly in his gaze, 'that Laura Nolan had no access to information, neither had Starky, but it had to look as if Starky had taken the information because it would save your neck. You, Senator, are the one who intended to give away the secrets, just as you have in the past.'

'You fool!' the Senator shouted.

'No, Senator,' Maddison retorted. 'The Russians knew too much, more than any single person in Medway Springs knew. They knew the results of the preliminary tests that Cape Kennedy had reported to you on Cusack's first shipment. That told the Russians just how vital the project was. Cusack didn't know – no one at Medway Springs knew, but you knew, Senator.'

'There were others,' the Senator snapped.

'But not at Medway Springs where Starky went through with his pantomime.'

'If what you say is true,' the Senator sneered, 'tell me why Starky took the photographs. Why did he take the risk of getting a copy of the report? Tell me that?'

'That, in fact, Senator, was your big mistake,' Maddison said calmly. 'McIntyre helped us out and a camera watched Starky all the time he was alone in the lab. Alone because you arranged that he would be so. You got Logan to assemble the scientists in his room, and you got your assistant to phone McIntyre. Starky took a photograph of his own report, not Cusack's and do you know why? Because you had got word to him that he had to use his camera. If he didn't use it we would know that there had been no leak. Starky used his camera and we got the signal but he took no photograph of Cusack's report. He only started the self-destroying mechanism timed to go off four hours later. Something that we purposely didn't tell you, Senator, so you couldn't tell Starky.'

The Senator's face was a mixture of confusion and rage.

'This is preposterous,' he shouted. 'Lies!'

'No, Senator,' Weiderman intervened. 'We have more evidence.'

'What do you mean?' the Senator said.

'McIntyre's reports for instance,' Weiderman replied.

'You got copies?'

'No, Senator, not all of the copies. You omitted to send us copies of McIntyre's reports which dealt with Laura Nolan. You thought McIntyre was in your power, Senator. What hold did you have over him? Was there some charge which you got him off the hook, when you were his Commanding Officer? Was there some incident?'

'Why don't you ask him?' the Senator snapped.

'I have and I know, Senator,' Weiderman replied. 'You thought McIntyre was well and truly one of your men. He owed you a couple of favours. You even got him fixed up after Korea. He wouldn't let you down. Well, Senator, he thought more about his country and his job. He began to wonder why the F.B.I. hadn't been called in sooner. Why you hadn't told them of his meeting with Laura Nolan. You see, Laura Nolan nearly confided in McIntyre, but you knew that, Senator, and you didn't tell us. Why?'

The Senator's face was ashen, his eyes cold and hard.

'You are going to have a hard fight on your hands, Weiderman,' he said acidly. 'All these accusations are going to have to be proved. I am an influential man. We are used to these investigations. We...'

'We?' Weiderman asked.

'Julius is a witness,' the Senator snapped. 'We'll make you fight every inch of the way. You don't know what you're letting yourself in for.'

'Senator,' Weiderman said calmly, 'I know how influential you are. You don't think I have let my men accuse you without careful investigation. Let me just tell you some more facts. First, Starky was not killed in the aeroplane. He is alive and under arrest. Diana Bradley is a disillusioned woman. She served your cause so long as someone served her. Starky was her reward. He

245

satisfied her, but he also ditched her. She thought she was meeting him in New York. Now she knows differently. Diana Bradley, Senator, is singing like a canary to save her neck, and so will Starky. As for you, Senator, do you honestly think we would let you go around the country shouting your head off, without having our watchdog?'

The Senator didn't reply.

'We've been very close to you for a long time, Senator, very close, and there are a number of large receipts of money which came into your election funds from suspicious sources. Oh! no, Senator, we know all about you. The game is up.'

If the Senator felt any tremor pass through his body he didn't show it, then.

'Am I under arrest?' he asked, tight lipped.

'Yes, Senator, you are,' Weiderman replied.

The Senator shrugged.

'You're going to look pretty stupid,' he said, but his voice had lost a lot of its former conviction.

Weiderman moved his head fractionally and two agents who had been standing close to the Senator, stepped forward and touched the Senator's arm.

'Do you mind if I take my lawyer with me?' the Senator asked.

Weiderman looked from the Senator to Stein and back again to the Senator.

'Sorry, Senator,' he said regretfully. 'I told you we had a man close to you. Julius is not your man. He is one of mine!'

This time the Senator did show his reactions. His mouth fell open and his knees visibly sagged. The two agents half lifted him out of the room. The Senator's world had collapsed around him.

When they were alone Weiderman said: 'Don't feel sorry for him. He is one of their very big fish. He could have gone far, very far. Fortunately the Russians are in too big a hurry to catch us up and fortunately we have had Julius working for us.' He turned to the dark faced, bespectacled Stein. 'You've done a very good job, Julius. A dirty, rotten job, but you've done it well. Thank you. I want your full report on my desk, first thing Monday morning.'

'Yes, Chief,' Stein said in his quiet voice, but his face had relaxed.

Weiderman turned to Maddison. 'Good work, Gary,' he said. 'I want you in Washington Monday. There's a plane Sunday evening.'

'Yes, Chief,' Maddison replied smiling.

'Now, come on, let's all have a drink,'

Weiderman said and produced another couple of bottles from a side cupboard. 'Hell! we deserve it.'

A couple of agents went over to Stein and gave him a glass. Suddenly the atmosphere relaxed. The room became noisy and smoky. Hugan collared Maddison.

'There are a lot of things that puzzled me,' he said, 'but one will do for now. When were you so sure Starky was one of them?'

'We suspected him from the beginning,' Maddison said. 'A hunch!' he smiled. 'When I looked at those snapshots in your house I was sure. People change over the years. You checked back on Starky, so did we. People recognised him. How? When we took a second look it was because Starky had visited Philadelphia and his old haunts last year. The Principal of the College was appointed ten years ago. He recognised Starky because Starky had called to see him. The same with the other people who identified him. Nobody recognised him from pre-war days. Starky had purposely prepared them for the day that someone might back check on him.'

'Good thinking,' the lieutenant said.

'And now here's one for you,' Maddison smiled.

'Fire away.'

'What made you go for Starky at the railroad station? You were pretty certain it wasn't him.'

'Yeah,' the lieutenant said proudly. 'I reckoned it was the Bradley dame.'

'How come?' Maddison asked.

'When we checked out all the cars for the lab boys we drew a blank, but we did find that the Bradley woman had a back rest in her driving seat. She liked to sit upright over the wheel. That keeper from the Club described the man driving the car as hunched up over the wheel. I figured it was either the Bradley dame in disguise or someone using her car. Bradley's alibi was watertight. She was at the dress rehearsal so it had to be someone using her car. I guessed it was Starky. When we trailed Starky to the station tonight, he was hunched up over the wheel. Starky didn't normally drive like that, but the Bradley woman did, so I figured it was the Bradley dame in disguise driving Starky's car.' The lieutenant gave one of his rare smiles. 'You see,' he added, 'Madge always drives with a cushion behind her back. That night we were sitting on the porch I watched her bring in the car. She was hunched up over the steering wheel.'

'That was a worthwhile drink we had,'

Maddison said.

'Yeah, it sure was, and it's time we had another.' The lieutenant grabbed the bottle. Sergeant Shean watched from the sideline. He had never seen the lieutenant so sociable before. 'Where's your glass, sergeant?' the lieutenant asked. The sergeant quickly found it.

The Saturday issue of the *Morning Star* enjoyed its largest circulation figures since the previous local election campaign. The arrest of Harry Starky and Diana Bradley on charges of first degree homicide was blazed across the front page in large, black print. The motive for the two murders was also boldly stated and it was this unveiled reference to a Communist power that made the people of Medway Springs sit up and take notice. It was then that they realised they were not just a town tucked away in the pine woods of Minnesota, but a town which had come under the eagle eye of the Kremlin. It was a disquieting thought.

Lieutenant Hugan was the hero of the day, and although reference was made to the F.B.I., the exact nature and extent of the Bureau's part was not revealed. Nor was reference made to the arrest of Senator

Leebright. That was something which was not due to hit the nation's headlines for a further four days, when Weiderman had his case so watertight as to convict the Senator of espionage. However, despite the suppression of this delicate piece of news, rumour of the Senator's arrest did reach the ears of Dr Logan and his associates. The rumour was greeted generally with little feeling of sympathy for the Senator, or concern. The Senator had not been a popular overlord. Only Hendrich and Helen Logan felt regret. Hendrich because he had been on the verge of cultivating the Senator's friendship and support, and had had visions of enjoying its fruits. It had cost him plenty. Now it was all wasted. However, Hendrich was relieved to think that there was no further fear of his visit to Ma Holling's brothel coming to light – at least not unless Emily decided to talk out of turn. An ace which Hendrich's wife intended to use to full advantage.

Helen Logan's regret at the rumour of the Senator's arrest was coupled with a similar reaction to that which Hendrich had felt when the stiff had been found in his lodge. She became afraid of what might come to light of her past friendship with the Senator!

The news of the arrest of Harry Starky

and Diana Bradley did surprise and shake the people with whom they had worked or been acquainted. Starky had been a popular figure and there was a certain amount of sympathy felt for him. Diana Bradley had few friends and few people felt sympathetic towards her.

On the Saturday evening Dr Logan's party, diminished in size with Starky's absence, still met as usual in the Country Club, when the main topic of conversation was naturally centred around the happenings of the past twenty-four hours. But nevertheless it turned out to be an unusually gay, lively evening. Dr Logan announced that he had sent his resignation to Washington and was accepting an appointment with the Chicago Chemical Plant. A position that he had been secretly negotiating over the past six months. The news of his resignation was greeted with vocal regret, but they were all aware that their group was about to split up. Dr Cusack was retiring and the other three scientists were to be invited to continue with their work at the space laboratory in Cape Kennedy. McIntyre had been commended by the F.B.I. on his high standard of security, and with the Senator now off his back, he looked a new man. He fully expected to be offered another similar appointment.

When Logan had earlier told his wife of his intention to take up a senior position with the Chicago Chemical Plant, he spelled out quite clearly what was going to be expected of her. He gave her a straight forward choice of either divorce or a closer relationship together. The Senator was not mentioned, neither was Kay, but Logan made it quite clear that any such future affairs were not acceptable. Helen Logan read the signs and knew that she was at a crossroad. Her husband was prepared to go it alone if necessary. She put off giving him a decision on the Saturday and intended to put it off indefinitely if possible, because it wasn't easy for Helen Logan to eat humble pie, or to admit to her husband that she was only attractive to other men so long as he was around to prop her up.

Maddison and Mary didn't join the party at the Country Club. Instead they spent the evening with Lieutenant Hugan and his wife. Madge Hugan had had a new hair do and looked radiant. She was exited about going out for the evening, and so was the lieutenant, who wondered why they hadn't done it more often. Maddison and Mary were happy just being together.

The publishers hope that this book has given you enjoyable reading. Large Print Books are especially designed to be as easy to see and hold as possible. If you wish a complete list of our books please ask at your local library or write directly to:

Dales Large Print Books
Magna House, Long Preston,
Skipton, North Yorkshire.
BD23 4ND